W9-BXA-215

Invisible Beasts

Invisible Beasts

Tales of the Animals that Go Unseen Among Us

Sharona Muir

Bellevue Literary Press
New York

First Published in the United States in 2014 by
Bellevue Literary Press, New York

FOR INFORMATION, CONTACT:
Bellevue Literary Press
NYU School of Medicine
550 First Avenue
OBV A612
New York, NY 10016

Library of Congress Cataloging-in-Publication Data
Muir, Sharona, 1957-
Invisible beasts : tales of the animals that go unseen among us / Sharona
Muir. — First edition.
pages cm
ISBN 978-1-934137-80-2 (pbk.) — ISBN 978-1-934137-81-9 (ebook)
1. Animals—Fiction. 2. Wildlife conservation—Fiction. I. Title.
PS3552.E5355I57 2014
813'.54—dc23   2013049256

Bellevue Literary Press would like to thank all its generous
donors—individuals and foundations—for their support.

Book design and composition by Mulberry Tree Press, Inc.

Manufactured in the United States of America.
FIRST EDITION

1   3   5   7   9   8   6   4   2
ISBN: 978-1-934137-80-2

Contents

Animal life is mindful, and the mind's life is animal.

Invisible Beasts

TALES OF THE ANIMALS THAT GO UNSEEN AMONG US

Introducing Invisible Beasts

I come from a long line of naturalists and scientists going back many generations, and in each generation we have had the gift of discovering hard-to-see phenomena, from a shelled amoeba lurking between two sand grains, to the misfolded limb of a protein pointing to a genetic flaw. This book also follows a venerable family tradition, but one never exposed to public view. Perhaps "trait" would be a better word than "tradition." Every so often, that is, every second or third generation, someone is born in our family who sees invisible animals. Our clan accepts the odd-sighted person without quibbles or qualms, in the spirit of generous tolerance and fun that animates the scientific community. In the late twentieth century, the odd-sighted arrival was myself. My induction into the family's attitude was typical. As a small child, I complained to my granduncle Erasmus—my predecessor, the elder spotter of invisible beasts—that since no one liked to go with me to catch invisible beetles, I wanted to see only what the other kids saw. From a height beclouded with cigar smoke, Granduncle rumbled, not unsympathetically:

"And what if Leeuwenhoek had wanted to see only what other people saw?" I retorted that Leeuwenhoek had had his microscope, but I couldn't make the other kids see what I saw. They didn't look hard enough. They didn't try, they didn't care, they laughed at me, and so forth. I must have sounded quite upset, because—like a monstrous barrier reef looming through brownish waters—the grand-avuncular mustache approached my face and stopped within a few inches, smelling of ashes and leather; I observed Granduncle's nostril hairs in the defile above his mustache, flying on his breath like pinfeathers.

"It's not how hard you look, Sophie. It's the way you see." A tusky yellow smile nailed these words to my mind. Decades later, they have led to this book.

Why have I written a book that could expose me, and my family, to ridicule and imputations of lunacy?

If the animals I saw weren't invisible, this book would not be unusual; it would be merely another in the current trend of wildlife catalogs. With the rate of species extinction at some four per hour, one hundred per day (according to Richard Leakey), how could we not create such projects as the online ARKive, where you may see and learn about the most imperiled animals? Mass extinction influenced me to write, especially because, for the first time, the family gift of seeing invisible beasts has not skipped a generation, but has descended directly to my nephew. I should have been Granduncle's age before meeting my replacement; and I suspect that this acceleration is linked, somehow, to the urgency of biological crisis.

But—you may ask—if these are my concerns, why strain

credibility by writing about phantoms? Why not join with other eco-minded citizens and write about saving the animals that we agree exist, because we can all see them?

To this reasonable question, I respond with my granduncle's words: it's in the way you see. I believe the time has come to share the way I see. That is, expressed in a nutshell: Human beings are the most invisible beasts, because we do not see ourselves as beasts. *If we did, we would think and act differently. Instead of believing ourselves to be above animals, or separate from them, we would understand how every aspect of our lives—spiritual, psychological, social, political—is, also, an aspect of our being animals. As it is, our understanding is superficial: everyone "knows" that he or she is a beast, yet how many of us ponder our animality, our condition of a creature among creatures, as we do our economy? We don't even have the proper words. Look at how* animal *and* beast *are used. Do you think you're a beast? Not really. Not you. I, however, seeing animals where no one else does, am that much more aware of our human blindness—a blind spot in our collective mind, roughly the size of the planet, that's turned on every creature including ourselves. Our distorted vision of life will only be corrected when we see the beasts that we don't see. How can we? For starters, read on.*

Some decisions should be explained. I have selected a limited number of invisible beasts out of the many that I have observed, as well as scores of others recorded by my granduncle and the beast spotters before him. A principle of selection was needed, but was hard to find. Entertainment? Any beast is as good as a circus—better, if you loathe circuses. Beauty? Not if the reader can't expect to see them. Oddity? Show me the animal that isn't surprising, and I'll show you a Disney film. Usefulness as pets? Not the Kraken. Finally, I decided to select those animals that taught me things I don't forget. Broadly put, the beasts you'll meet here are those who teach a memorable lesson in the meaning of their particular company to the human animal.

Another decision was to include more personal details than usual in a catalog of natural wonders. Without anecdotal touches, I would not be able to explain, for instance, why it's a misfortune when your Truth Bats desert you, or how I solved the riddle of invisible dogs. My family enters the picture as well. My younger sister, Evie, is a biologist specializing in soil science. Without her expert assistance, I couldn't begin to describe the lives of invisible creatures. Evie's enthusiasm is as helpful as her knowledge; she truly enjoys treating invisible beasts as biological thought experiments. She is a natural part of the book, especially since her son, Leif, is this century's successor to Granduncle Erasmus and me.

The hardest decisions involved organization. How should the animals be named? Greco-Latin taxonomies were out, because those require generations of systematics by people who see what you see. So all names are informal, and I've classified the creatures according to my best guesses about the kinships between visible and invisible life. The same goes for

*the categories: common, rare, and imperiled. These are pro-
visional, drawn from long-range observations by me and
my predecessors, like population estimates made by a few
researchers working in a remote jungle or desert. As with all
my conclusions, the categories await scientific verification. I
wish to present invisible beasts to the reader without making
unwarranted claims; I merely claim my practice to be that
of a naturalist, and hope that my descriptions may someday
assist in a more scientific approach to this fascinating subject.*

How, then, is the book organized?

*My inspiration comes from sunflowers, whose seeds grow
in a spiral progression called the Fibonacci series. This book's
chapters take the form of a diminishing Fibonacci series: 8,
5, 3, 2, 1, 1, like the spiral of a sunflower disk (a very young
one!) traced inward, taking the reader from a periphery of
common invisible beasts, through shrinking circles of imperiled, rare, and others types of beasts, to the central mysteries
pondered in the epilogue. Now, the Fibonacci series is one
of those mathematical doohickeys, like constants and ratios,
that nature seems to carry in her overall pockets and keep
handy for routine work. Both scientists and artists use it on
occasion, and in its small domain of tasks, the series is not a
bad symbol of modest, all-around utility. So let the order of
the chapters before you represent my chief wish for this book,
modeled after a growing sunflower or paper nautilus: that it
be found useful.*

Common Invisible Beasts

I

We can solve many problems in life by imitating the ways of fellow creatures: this is called "biomimicry." Engineers are biomimics when they study animals, learning from scorpions how to make erosion-proof surfaces, or, from octopi, how to design superior camouflage. Biomimicry is not limited to science, however; we can be biomimics with our imaginations and feelings, too. The Couch Conch teaches as much about love and marriage as it does about durable materials.

The Couch Conch

A NIGHT OF PASSION is a hard thing to remember (no pun intended.) The moments blur into a warm blush on your brain, from which it's hard to extract the details later, if you want to brood over them and confirm just how he did what. So it's lovely to find a Couch Conch in your bedroom the morning after.

You know when a Couch Conch is spending the night from the atmosphere it diffuses. Your limbs loosen; you have the most marvelous sense of relaxing on some sandy bottom among beds of warm sea grass in tropical waters. Your lover tastes like fresh oysters and tart wine; his kisses are iridescent, plentiful, while your toes fan apart and wave hungrily. Gravity is suspended for the night as you spiral deeper into spellbound synchrony, warm and wet. His looks are swimming with love, his hand tangles in your hair, his navel is adorable, like a blister pearl, and swells toward your smiling face with each deep breath sounding like the sea, which is the sound of "pink noise" . . . as it's well-named, since the pink lips of conches waft that same noise to our eardrums.

But, as I said, you find your Couch Conch in the morning after all the delights are past, perched beside the clock radio. And unlike the souvenir shell held to your head in an airport gift shop, the Couch Conch isn't empty. It is bowing on its foot. You might say hello, or something.

Like its visible kin, a Couch Conch seems the symbol of a perfect union. Its feminine, rosy lip is borne along in eager leaps by its foot, which my dictionary describes as "pointed and horny," and this hot foot obtrudes from an *operculum*, which is Latin for "lid." Gazing at your Couch Conch, you hear Nature saying in her peremptory way that every pot has its lid, so get busy and find yours! As if that weren't enough of a hint, most conches unfurl their gorgeous, pouting lips—so reminiscent of our bodies at sexual maturity—at *their* sexual maturity.

That's when a Couch Conch pays its visit to your boudoir. As you gently lift the Couch Conch from your nightstand, careful not to jar its squirming foot—which probes your wrist for plankton, pathetically—you see what makes this creature unique. Its gleaming lip sports ornate and delicate carvings; in the film of pale shell that overlays its radiant pink, there's an ecstatic face with tousled locks, framed by a pair of hands. In a rondure of magenta, standing nudes, white with passion, dig fingers into each other's rumps. Two lovers are glued in a leggy X, staring at each other. They look like naughty Victorian cameos. In fact the Couch Conch's cameos, which it acquires at puberty, are a natural enhancement to attract mates, much as body piercings or tattoos mark our own debuts. But there's another surprise in store. Slipping on your glasses, the better to scrutinize, you bend closer to your kelp-smelling visitor and gasp. You've just seen what you look like upside down, in the buff.

Fortunately for your dignity, the Couch Conch is not a camera. The cameos are made by another process, requiring heat rather than light (see below) and possess a personal aura, the *je ne sais quoi* of a genuine artwork. A camera shows naked bodies that you see: the Couch Conch shows naked moments that you recognize. There's the moment, stunning, when his finger traced your tense lower lip, which unfairly makes you look thin-lipped because it holds back an avalanche of worries about how you aren't young enough, thin enough, rich enough, smart enough, and just plain not enough. Your lover saw, laughed, touched, and your poor mouth relaxed. You thought you had been smiling, but only at his magic touch did a smile unfold that you could feel. What a full lip is silhouetted here, in your smile! Now you can put your finger on the memory.

It's wonderful that mollusks, who don't care about us, can show us what our bodies express. But mollusks are full of lessons. They know all about the balance of hard and soft, rigidity and acceptance, firmness and flexibility, from the way in which they compose their nacre, the iridescent glaze that makes pearls precious and conches beautiful. We don't think of beauty in terms of incredible toughness, but it so happens that nacre, that angelic gloss, is damn near unbreakable. It's made of hard crystals and gooey, soft protein. If a crack starts running through the rigid crystals, it stops dead in the yielding goo. Isn't that worth studying if you're a human couple?

We humans make an inferior commercial copy of nacre, by sintering. I'm guessing you don't sinter much. It requires temperatures of around 2000 Celsius. Conches make the real article, which we can't imitate, while lolling in beds of sea grass with no more heat than puberty calls for, and with no more wasted effort than the lilies whose folded white genitals trumped Solomon in all his glory.

Now, as for the naughty cameos, nothing could be simpler. The Couch Conch's protein goo is heat sensitive, like infrared film. Our body heat impresses itself on this protein, and as the Couch Conch completes its shell lip, the goo "develops" the heat-images of our ecstasies three-dimensionally by contracting and expanding various layers of crystals. This isn't hard to grasp. It's exactly as if a 3-D digital modeling program were a marine life-form with a slimy foot that hung out in people's bedrooms while they canoodled, then mysteriously vanished around nine in the morning, leaving a fishy whiff and a smear of sand, on its way to find a bodacious *Strombus gigas* and spawn some glutinous egg strands.

2

*C*an nonhumans be artists? I suppose "art" is a human concept, yet anyone who has heard a mockingbird singing under a spring moon has heard an animal out-riff Bird; it's hard to believe they do it without some aesthetic sense. Like ours, the works of nonhumans have individuality. I've seen many competent webs made by arrow-shaped micrathena spiders, but only one that was perfectly round, with strands spun as evenly as the grooves in an LP, and not by accident—for it was remade many times—but by the mastery of a single spider. The Feral Parfumier Bees show how animals can make a thing of beauty following a procedure well known to human artists.

Feral Parfumier Bees

On a cold spring night in the Pleistocene, in the midst of forests rubbing like bear pelts against the flinty stars, a bolt of lightning locked onto heaven and earth and staggered in its violent light that froze an entire horizon of shadows. Minutes later, a banner of fire unfurled, smoked, and sank under rainy gusts. In its place lay the ruins of a pitch pine, still hissing, alive with crawling sparks. Some chunks of pine had exploded off the burning boughs, showering hot ash, and smacked into the undergrowth like arboreal meteorites. One had rolled into the mouth of a dire-wolf den whose occupants were out hunting. Bumping downward, smutched with wolf hairs, jiggling from residual steam in its pitch that jetted it first one way, then the other, it sped over claw-marked dirt and fell ten feet, *whoosh*, down a crack leading from the wolves' den into the true pores of the earth. It landed in a pocket of rock as a pinball lands in its hole, and there, with mass subsiding and heat sighing away, it rested for twenty-five millennia.

At first, the thread of steamy incense unraveling at the back of the den caused anxious sniffing from the mother of four dire puppies, who all grew up safely but never experienced, in hundreds of miles of travels, a fragrance anything like their home den's. Eventually, the den lost the incense smell and, forever, the scent of dire wolves. Gray wolves, red wolves, and timber wolves took their place for a span of time equal to the lives of empires; then coyotes, foxes, groundhogs, and skunks (thanks to the spread of a human empire) overran the burrows of the wolves. By this time the innumerable pines that had bristled in the cold spring lightning were mostly flattened into rivers of asphalt. But the ancient, charred chunk—a great artwork waiting for its audience—stayed intact through the eons, slowly hardening. I should say a word about it.

It was unique. Before being coated in molten pitch, it had clung to a pine branch onto which it exuded a shiny ooze meant to repel weaver ants, though there were no weaver ants anywhere around. It didn't know that. It clung to its spot: a rough sphere that from a short distance gave the impression of fruitlike translucence, varying with the sunbeams from rosy-peach to yellow amber. Up closer—from the perspective of a giant ground sloth—it got strange. The sloth had no concept of "beehive," much less "hexagon," though a golden ball composed of Tiffany-like translucent grids gave him as much pause as could be sustained by a hungry, incurious guy with claws like personal forklifts. One thing the sloth knew: it smelled *good.*

The next thing he knew, he was galloping about on his massive knuckles, making the sound (whatever it was) of *Eremotherium* harassed by wasps. He felt wasps, he heard wasps, wasps stung his ears, drilled up his snout, stabbed at his bony little eyes—but he didn't see any wasps. He left in a hurry anyway. And a defensive swarm of invisible honeybees returned to crawl over their comb in four-bee-thick cosiness, though they had no business to be (or bee) in North America. But they didn't know that.

These bees were naive newcomers. Their comb, scarcely secreted into place, came there by sheer accident. Natural selection can magnify an accident into a new variation on the theme of life, or let it dwindle into extinction. For all our bees' sloth-banishing activity, they had little defense against dangers like bears—those Pleistocene bears tall enough to have ambled into your house and scratched their chins on top of your Christmas tree. And they had no defense against a North American winter. They were running out of time.

Invisible, or Parfumier, Bees are natives of Asia, where they likely sprang from the oldest lineage of honeybees, the red-bellied dwarf honeybee, *Micrapis florea*. Though noble in their antiquity, *Micrapis* have never been the brightest bees on the planet—they never learned to waggle-dance, for example. Our invisible *Micrapis*, marooned on a cold, alien continent, never considered sheltering in a cave or hollow tree. Dim aristocrats that they were, they built on a pitch-pine limb the same

fragile pavilion that suited their queen in the home latitudes of cinnamon, vetiver, and pepper. They danced their
same, waggle-less, straitlaced beeline, pointing to nectar
sources of which they knew absolutely nothing. Out and
back they flew, and one can only imagine the discomfort
of this genteel sisterhood on finding their honeys and jel-
lies altered beyond repair. Everyone performed her duty:
the foragers danced, the cleaners swept and garnished,
the porters ported, the nurses nursed, and the queen's
attendants licked her constantly and sped her commands
to the colony. Yet nothing smelled right. Their beautiful
comb, that sweet home epitomizing the best of vigorous
feminine care, reeked of poor levulose levels and unpleas-
ant ratios of copper to manganese. Social insects all agree
that life bows to a well-executed plan, so the Parfumiers,
confronted with seeping evil, continued to do what they
did best, with emphasis. They ranged farther; gathered
more data; memorized new landmarks. They pioneered!
Veteran foragers—bees of experience, whose antennae
alerted to the slightest trace of sugar, who could sniff
the very hour at which a flower had unfolded—these
exquisitely discriminating Parfumiers got their tongues
trapped in heavy-duty, spring-loaded sepals meant for
the oversize jabs of hummingbirds. They hauled the icy-
tasting pollens of the temperate zone. They scaled saber-
toothed roses, mandibular violets, grasses that could saw
through a glacier's toes. They were as brave as brides.

Yet despite exceptional industry, the honey of the

stranded Parfumiers smelled more and more odd. It nourished them, roughly, but somewhere in its aromatic heart lurked an indigestible dissonance, where the chemistries of received wisdom wrestled with the nectars of circumstance. And their time was running out, though they didn't know that.

They knew the supreme truth of bees: honey is collaboration. The taste of honey is the taste of sisterhood. Everybody involved in making honey has to agree about such technical matters as the quality standard, when to stop regurgitating the refined product, how long to fan off the excess water, and so on, with many other decisions we're not aware of as we pour the stuff all over our granola. Unlike us, bees have a sound mass mind, so good at collective decisions that they don't even need to be conscious of them. It is also a mind capable of abstract thought. Bees know the concepts of *sameness* and *difference*, and the Parfumiers, in their rude spring of exile, had brought home a string of unknown ingredients, one after another, trying to make their honey the *same* as it used to be. Their approximations tasted like approximations, but each was slightly *different* from the one before. Then something extraordinary happened, simply because it had to. A point came when the Parfumiers' honey wasn't a failed version of the same one they used to make, but a whole new thing. I couldn't say if the Parfumiers' mass mind consciously read out a royal proclamation to the effect of "Our honey is not the same—then let it be different." But anyone, even a social insect, who tries to realize a plan through successive approximations is eventually bound to realize not the plan itself, but the sum of the differences between plan and reality. That is the procedure of artists, and the invisible bees, working with unknown materials, had produced a great artwork of the olfactory senses. No one could have identified its resemblances to a flower, or even a potpourri of several flowers. Nothing in nature had smelled like it before. Imagine, however, some unlucky person who would die without ever having encountered a flower, a person whose footfalls regularly met cement, whose raised eyes bumped off a dead layer of clouds, whose hopes consisted of daily crusts, and whose fears were so familiar they couldn't be bothered to wear faces. Smelling the Parfumiers' honey, that sad soul would know precisely what a flower was and what it meant—the heart of change that makes hope possible. Our bees had become like the invisible sisterhood of the Muses: their honey was pure poetry.

BEWARE GREATNESS! Like all art of the highest order, the Parfumiers' unmasked, gently but implacably, our human imperfection. It happened this way:

Twenty-five millennia after a pitch-coated honeycomb fell into a hole under a dire-wolf den, I was enjoying a bright spring morning. I was buttering toast. Patches of sunlight danced on the kitchen counter, where a smudge of raspberry jam drew a bee through the open window—she flew past my ear, grazing it with her hot hum. My other ear pressed to the cell phone, I listened to my sister Evie. Most people's voices saw up and down when they're excited, but Evie's voice separates into identically-sized syllables all simmering at the same high, maximally efficient pitch, like water heated in a warm pan until convection bubbles, those exactly hexagonal bubbles, cover the surface and simmer according to the same laws of physics that command hexagonal cells in a beehive. I think it's nice for a biologist's voice to exhibit one of nature's fundamental patterns. My sister was telling me about a honeycomb, miraculously preserved from the Pleistocene, complete with the bodies of an unknown, primitive species of *Micrapis*.

"'My crap is'?"

"*Apis*, bee, *micro*, small, Sophie! Anyway, my graduate student has been running this mummified honeycomb through batteries of tests," Evie continued, her tone implying that I was intellectually limp though still good enough for her news. She and her student had built models of the dead bees through digital simulation, and, finally, had synthesized a replica of the ancient honey, based on melissopalynological and paleobiochemical analysis. Typically, Evie pronounced these terms without lessening the rate and pitch of her speech. She invited me to visit her lab.

"It's super-incredible. Wait till you smell it."

"Smell what?"

"You won't believe your nose."

POSTERS OF BRIGHTLY DYED microorganisms, like creepy crawly clerestory windows, decorated the door to Evie's lab. My baby sister was perched on her swivel chair, at her sprawling bench. Her bangs flipped joyfully at the ends of her sentences. Before I got to see her digitally simulated bee, she insisted that I take a sniff of the reconstructed Pleistocene honey.

"This isn't a prank? It's not some kind of drug?"

"I would never give an already crazy person a drug. Come on," she coaxed, handing me a sealed Pyrex retort, its interior coated in small brown beads.

I put my nostril, as instructed, to a tube hanging from the retort, pressed a tiny plastic catch, inhaled, and let out a long whistle. I pressed the catch again, and again, eyes closed, drawing the fragrance into my memory as hard as I could. "That's enough," Evie warned. "We have to limit its exposure. Sorry—I know it's tempting."

"Don't you think . . . it smells a bit like . . . Joy?" I asked.

"Smells like freakin' paradise."

I explained that Joy is a perfume, and Evie shrugged.

"How would I know about French perfumes, with the gorilla I'm married to? Let me show you this bee . . ." She brushed the computer keys. On the monitor, the bee's foot-long image was reddish and furry. Magnified again, her fur resembled tangles of raspberry cane. "The branched hairs mean she was a good sticky pollen collector. But what was she doing here, Sophie? Honeybees didn't arrive on this continent till the Pilgrims brought them, and they sure didn't bring *Micrapis*. That's an Asian bee."

I looked at the bee, then at my sister, temporarily unable to speak. Scientists are animals too, and if you trigger their instincts, you have only yourself to blame. Images flew past on the monitor; Evie was scouting for a scent.

I was thinking of the Keen-Ears. They are a thriving species of invisible humans, and some of their clans live in caves in my woods. The Keen-Ears tolerate me as a harmless snoop; they don't understand why I've posted signs on their perimeter and check it daily, with my dog, for evidence of trespass. They have no idea how I've fought on zoning boards to keep their habitat untouched, and their existence unsuspected. Unworried, they go about their invisible business, tending their red, furry bees that made the dangerous trek with them— preceding *Homo sapiens* by some twelve millennia—out of Asia, across the frigid marshes of Beringia, and down into a land of giant bears and sloths, a lonesome immensity where (as their mournful ballads recount) a beating human heart sounded as loud as thunder and lightning.

The Keen-Ears would not know what I did now. I was making a decision.

Evie lacked one clue to solve her mystery, and it was

this: when they die, *invisible beasts become visible.* (Their bodies go unnoticed, blending into the endless ranks of unknown species.) With that clue, Evie would realize what her Asian bee was, and how it had come to America in the bee-baskets of the primordial Keen-Ears. One word from me, and science could open the vaults of invisible life.

But what would happen to animals impossible to see until they died? The outlook was not good. Humans are not like bees; we did not evolve from predatory wasps into dancing, vegetarian beings whose honey tastes of sisterhood. Humanity's first reaction to the news would be to go out and kill—kill what we couldn't see and didn't understand. Before my mind's eye rolled a vision of Keen-Ear bodies flung in heaps, tied to truck fenders, stuffed and mounted as trophies. I imagined the TV talk shows and the shrieking Web. I imagined the Keen-Ear survivors, sad toys of defense research, dragging on their lives in sunless laboratories. As for their Parfumier Bees . . . as colonies of visible honeybees went on collapsing, some entrepreneur would doubtless try to farm the invisibles, God help them. Or they might go feral again, in a world ridding itself of wild bees. These horrors were the likeliest result of giving Evie the clue she lacked.

Yet I owed my sister. She had never belittled my invisible beasts; no, she had always helped me to understand them. She was a cherished guide on the obscure track I pursued in life. And I owed science a debt, too, for giving me, since childhood, my inspiration and a standard of truth.

That is what I imagined, and pondered, while Evie knitted her brows and gazed at her computer screen.

"This bee of yours," I said, steadying my voice, "it's extinct, of course."

"Well, look at it—it's practically a wasp. It's not far from its wasp progenitors, and it's very, very far from a modern bee. I can't imagine it's still around. But," Evie said, nailing me with a look, "nature is usually about what we can't imagine."

3

Here (with apologies to Evie) I describe the Keen-Ears, an invisible human subspecies with unusual gifts, whose clans I am privileged to shelter in my woods. The most memorable lesson I've learned from them concerns an ancient problem that our species share, and that they approach by emulating ants—no, it's not about hard work or planning ahead . . .

The Keen-Ears

We humans are not alone. A few subspecies of our kind survive in the dangerous company of *Homo sapiens* by being invisible. The Keen-Ears live in woodlands east of the Rockies and cultivate the edible tree fungus *Laetiporus*, or chicken-of-the-woods, which causes wood rot but is considered a delicacy by both visible and invisible humans. The Keen-Ears are master fungus breeders; they create many invisible strains of *Laetiporus*, puzzling some foresters, who can see that a log is rotting, all right, but cannot see why. Visible *Laetiporus* looks like an orange brain. In the invisible varieties, the Keen-Ears have bred a palette of colors—teal, mauve, scarlet, ice pink, purple—in concentric, paisley, striped, and marbled designs. Wisely, the Keen-Ears have tampered with visible *Laetiporus* to keep it from breeding with its glamorous invisible cousins. They don't want any episodes of *Homo sapiens* stumbling onto a psychedelic fungus protruding from a tree trunk, finding out why, then killing or enslaving all the Keen-Ears. With some remorse—because they're serious about

bioethics and believe in sharing the benefits of science—
the Keen-Ears think they are justified in keeping their
fungus farming secrets from us. They think we mostly pre-
fer mushrooms, anyway.

The Keen-Ears are short, slight, furred, and have large
ears that make them look like Hermes in his winged hel-
met. Their fur is gray and weather-resistant, so they go
naked, with a double pelt in winter. Their ears are so keen
that they can hear blood coursing through the body's vessels. Not even the Great Horned Owl can float by them
unnoticed; they hear its pulse beating over the treetops as
it readies the mouse-sized cage of its claws. This special
gift has countless ramifications, most of them enviable.

Among the Keen-Ears, you never see two people trying to move out of each other's way, apologizing as they
both step right or left at the same time. The Keen-Ears
can detect the sound of muscles tensing for a movement—like dogs, they can tell when you're about to get
up, or leave the room. At mealtimes, eerily, they share a
salt dip without a word or glance from the person offering or accepting. What's more, each person has a blood-
signature which sounds as unique to them as a voice to
us. A Keen-Ear lying with eyes closed under a feather
blanket knows exactly which child is creeping barefoot
to the fried fungus jar. They also hear the turbulence
that anger causes, and know the combinations of blood-
sound and body language for a wide range of feelings.
Living as they do in small clans, their minds are nearly as

naked as their bodies. (This makes fistfights challenging, though feasible.) They sometimes talk on algae-powered telephones, but such bloodless communication is called "corpse talk" and viewed as an unseemly necessity.

They have epic songs about the dangers awaiting small, isolated genetic groups like their own clans. The verses they intone, while doing chores in their caves, tell of beasts who selected themselves into an evolutionary cul-de-sac, or outgrew their niches. The Keen-Ears don't particularly enjoy these mournful lays, but insist that their daily performance is vital to "good health." They call us "Flu-huggers," and say that we have poor bodily health because we don't sing the tales of the species gone from our habitats. Curiously, the Keen-Ears' songs really do help them prevent disease. The ancient melodies were composed to harmonize with the bloodstream—with the boom of stretched atria or the arpeggios of squeezed capillaries—and the Keen-Ears "play" their blood pressure like an instrument, through biofeedback, while singing. This is very good for their hearts. They also diagnose vascular illness with astonishing precision. From eavesdropping on their gossip, for instance, I learned about my illness long before a doctor noticed anything—"that old snoop with arterial plaque," they called me. (Admittedly, I see the Keen-Ears more often than doctors.)

The sheer physical harmony of the Keen-Ears' lives seems to limit antagonism. When five of them sit on a twisted oak-root to peruse a map of fungus stands, they sink onto it as one, gracefully. Nobody has to scoot over or scrunch in. It's not surprising that they dance like angels and make love with the ease of the elements. But for all that, the Keen-Ears are human, and for them as for us, love is complication.

Versed in fungus genetics and animal genealogies, the Keen-Ears have long ago mastered the art of breeding themselves; but unlike us, who try such things under the spur of creepy racism, the Keen-Ears enjoy a personal and sexual freedom we can scarcely imagine, coupled with social stability. Their folkways, though unsuitable for our own rambunctious, high-strung species, are yet worthwhile to contemplate. They live in clans separated by gender. Between men's and women's caves there is plenty of traffic, and all relationships are possible—business, cultural collaborations of all kinds, professional associations, friendships, love affairs, even hauntingly coordinated orgies. But when it comes to making babies, each women's clan hosts one male guest, who is the exclusive father of any infants born during his stay. After about three years, he rejoins his old clan and the women choose a new man. Genealogies are closely tracked. To prevent inbreeding, a clan father is never invited twice, and incestuous ties are taboo. Sons go to live with their father's clan in late childhood, but both sons and daughters remain in close touch with their biological parents and siblings. Careful family planning, and tight family and clan ties, mean that no one in the

Keen-Ear caves is born unwanted, or dies untended, or lives in poverty—and everybody babysits. How many times I've lurked outside a warmly lit Keen-Ear cave, wistfully eavesdropping on conversations in which these precious safeguards are taken for granted.

The marriage rite of the Keen-Ears is the most exotic part of their family arrangements. To choose clan fathers, they have adapted a process of decision-making found among ants and bees.

"It's time you learned about the ants and the bees," Keen-Ear parents tell their children, clearing their throats. Particularly ants. The lesson sends little Keen-Ear girls scurrying to find anthills, spending hours in rapturous observation, as our own small daughters play at becoming brides. The naughtiest Keen-Ear girls even kick apart anthills for the secret thrill of watching the great event happen. Called "quorum sensing," the process helps ants and bees choose new nesting sites without having to rely on an authority—a judge, boss, or chief— to make the final decision. It begins with scouts; in the case of ants, each scout goes off separately to find a new possible nest site, then scurries back to the colony, delivers a report, and recruits other ants to visit the potential site. Timing is the key to the final decision: ants reporting an inferior site take a little longer, as if mastering some embarrassment, and the delay ultimately counts, as we will see. Though trickles of hurried ants running in and out of rocky crevices may not sound romantic, nothing could be more breathlessly fascinating than the marriage rite of the Keen-Ears, those wise apes of the ants!

In spring, when the moon shining through translucent leaves suspends the black trees in a jelly of light, and flowering crabapples perfume the night, the Keen-Ear women dust their bodies with colored powders, hang strings of oak-pollen tassels from their ears to their glimmering shoulders, and fasten filigree capes, made of leaf-skeletons, from their necks to their ankles. In this ceremonial dress, all the women—from old, bent clan mothers clinging to a youngster's elbow, to young would-be mothers standing very straight with excitement—visit the candidates for clan fatherhood, who have spent months preparing for the events of this evening, called Niche Night.

It's not a tryst, nobody is going to bed—at least, that's the official version. This meeting is supposed to be a formal interview, taking place in a rocky niche reserved for the event. The candidate has to show that he can get along with all those eager, fussy females, young and old, who want his genes, his affection, his company, and his help around the cave. His aim is to attract as many of the women as possible to his niche, because the number of visitors will, in the end, decide the outcome of his candidacy.

For a first-time candidate, preparing for Niche Night is a grueling rite of passage. Once he has fathered and helped to rear babies, he will have established himself as a Keen-Ear parent, and may be invited, during his life, to several women's caves. But he has to be picked that crucial first time. The stress is on. He spends weeks researching the clans whose women are likely to visit: their environs, personalities, problems, projects. If he has a girlfriend in the clan, he begs for advice till her ears are ringing. He pumps his female relatives and friends for gossip—do these women like pets? Should he offer a nest of phoebes for their cave ledge? Will it bug them if he cracks his knuckles? He asks his father what made him successful. His father shrugs, and pats him on the back. His mother says, Be Yourself. His sisters laugh. His brothers are all pretending that they know where the best niches are, the ones with waterfall views, but maybe they'll tell him and maybe they won't. For days, he has practiced serving up fermented acorn liqueur with a suave flourish. He has memorized compliments, jokes, soulful sayings, earnest platitudes, and poetry. He has placed his great-great-grandfather's Pluricorn horn armlet, a priceless icebreaker, where it cannot escape notice.

Quorum sensing begins, as I've said, with scouts. Ants send scouts to look at nest sites; the Keen-Ear women send scouts to interview the male candidates. What really happens between the scouts and the candidates is the subject of many jokes and folktales. After all, the Keen-Ears are only human. And though they go naked, a Keen-Ear lady wearing nothing but a netted cape and earrings is not naked, she is fetchingly nude, while a well-set-up Keen-Ear man wearing nothing but warm intentions and yesterday's love-bites is a force to be reckoned with. The oldest joke about the unofficial aspect of Niche Night goes:

"If two women walk into your cave, which one is the scout?"

"The one walking bowlegged." There are the Three Honored Scouts, a famous trio in song and smut: the drunk scout, the bowlegged scout, and the scout who is old, drunk, and bowlegged, and always gets the punch line. But at least in public, Keen-Ears don't admit to hanky-panky on Niche Night.

While the scouts interview the candidates, the other Keen-Ear ladies lounge around the cave, biting their lips, telling stories, playing cards, yawning. The middle-aged women who run everything and everybody confer in low tones, broken by bawdy cackles. The oldest ladies look at each other with rueful nostalgia and quaver, "I hope those boys have a feather roll for my feet." Time elapses, and the lapsed time is the key to the whole process.

As the scouts report back, the wisdom of ants becomes apparent. A Keen-Ear girl reappears in the cave entrance and immediately, the sound of her blood thunders like a snowmelt cataract in everyone's ears and they cheer, gathering round to hug the scout as she weeps happy tears, speaking the lucky candidate's name. Another scout returns on the first one's heels, her blood thrumming pleasantly like muffled snare drums. This raises smiles, but also questions: so, what was not to like? She is badgered for details, analysis—a full report, in time-consuming words. Meanwhile, a third scout rushes in, her blood roaring like a forest on fire, her ears flapping with haste, and the clan breaks into applause. By the time the second scout has persuaded a couple of women to visit the nice-but-not-perfect fellow, many others are on their way to or from the first and third scouts' fabulous men—it's only natural, enthusiasm is infectious. More scouts come in, and the ones whose blood does not speak volumes instantly, who have to give verbal answers, take longer to report and recruit fewer ladies to visit their candidates. As the night wears on, the number of women trekking to and from a particular candidate's niche reveals who the best choice must be. It is obvious to everyone. No need for an authority to dictate anything. The Keen-Ear women vote with their hearts, their sharp ears, and their feet.

These customs look outlandish to visible humans like you and me—cold-blooded, conformist, full of potential disasters, dystopian, and rather crass. But suppose we imagine them a little differently? Suppose the male candidates were all the different aspects of one person, and the visiting women were all the different aspects of another person? Quorum sensing is very much like the way we instinctively select the aspects of our mates that suit us best. Over time, as we get to know each other, some aspects will draw us again and again by well-trodden paths, while others will be less visited. Our wives and husbands, partners and lovers, the very people closest to us, are crowded with unknown personalities. But our time together is limited, so we cannot learn them all. We scarcely have time to know ourselves. We stick to a little circle of familiar faces, and are surprised when a new acquaintance speaks up from the pillow, or a stranger offers a cool nod. Now does Niche Night seem more familiar? The Keen-Ears and the "Flu-huggers" share an ancient human problem: love is too big a task for our allotted time.

4

*A*nyone can see an invisible beast once it's dead. Usually, though, the opportunity arises on the roadways after the invisible animal has been squashed flat, and nobody stops to inspect it. Biologists sometimes notice the odd corpse, but take it for a specimen of yet another unknown (visible) species; after all, according to the National Geographic, some 86 percent of living species have yet to be described. Viewed in this light, the discovery described here was serendipitous.

The Pluricorn

The driver of a Ford pickup spotted something antler-shaped in the breakdown lane. He pulled over, expecting a tasty hoard of venison. What he found instead, he photographed and posted on the Web with the caption "Dead Dinosaur Deer." The posting drew comments from the scurrilous to the reflective from hunters, bone hunters, and information gatherers.

"Faking a giant rack is just one of those things a real man doesn't do," quipped a hunter. A paleontologist posted an earnest plea not to spread dinosaur hoaxes, as they bolstered antiscientific prejudice in the American public. Evie sent me the link with a note: "Pluricorn?"

The photo did resemble a Pluricorn. They live in my woods, and I know no other animal whose males are so patently designed for misery. The best sketch I've made of a specimen was typical—a young male, nibbling hawthorn leaves. He was especially pitiable in May, when other species are showing off their renewed beauty and spirits. As I strolled on one of my trails, illumined by new green mists in the boughs of the oaks and ash trees, I saw signs of creaturely grace everywhere. Two red fox pups who lived in a rockpile were sunning and stretching, rumps raised, heads low, tails flourished like new ferns, and on the other end, pink tongues outfurled like petals. A mother Cooper's hawk, meat in her beak, flew toward her nest through tangled branches as if they melted before her. The very ground lost its dullness where grape hyacinths and violets spread like gaps of sky. And from the throats of toads who resembled clods, issued a sweet trilling chorus that swelled like woodwinds, sank, swelled again, and never ceased.

Into this charming scene came the wretched Pluricorn. The moment I spotted him—a movement of sundapples cohering, the way it does, into an animal shape—I knew the reason for certain bizarre rub marks on the hawthorns that earlier had puzzled me. This beast was too hungry to care about my lurking presence. Craning into the leafage, he sported a barbed brow horn, a fringe of curly tusks, a horn projecting from his chest, and big spurs, like ivory artichokes, on his rather knock-kneed legs. Over his head, a massive rack cast a grotesque, thorny shadow. Poor beast, he kept bashing himself on the hawthorn trunk, or tipping too far to one side and pawing rapidly to adjust. My stomach hurt to see him; how was he going to feed all four of his? Sketching him quickly on my notepad, I analyzed the details afterward.

Chinese water deer have tusks, though fewer than the Pluricorn. Most of his equipment looks like antler tissue gone berserk, but his leg spurs look like naked bone protruding from under his skin. That has to hurt. Pathologies come to mind, galloping bone cancers ... Such airy speculation embarrasses me, though, since without proper scientific study, I have no proof that the Pluricorn is a deer at all. Marco Polo once wrote a fine description of a unicorn that he'd actually seen, which happened to be a rhinoceros. For all I know, the Pluricorn is a very unusual crab. Science alone can settle this question. Tempting as it is to throw up one's hands, however, I cannot leave the subject without an educated guess. I would guess that the Pluricorn is struggling down a rough evolutionary road, having taken an unlucky turn a long time ago. Here is a plausible scenario.

Imagine an autumn day in the Pleistocene epoch, steamy with thunderstorms. Male *Cervidae* are in a mood to spar and mate. In sight of the does, two lusty young Pluricorns square off. They paw, snort, and charge each other like jousting knights. The does' ears flicker like the sleeves of medieval ladies-in-waiting. Some time elapses. After a while the does trot delicately into a circle around the males. The two champions are lying on the ground completely tangled up, heaving and trying to snort, tusks Velcroed to tusks, antlers locked, leg spurs enmeshed, and barbs, well, just adding to the mess. Some hours pass like this. Lightning crackles, rain sluices down, the males glare pitifully from their mutual fetters. Meanwhile, the houri-eyed does stand about in the rising mists of the afternoon, nostrils aquiver, absorbing a message from their genes. It says that these rutting males are not the only rutting males in the Pleistocene. And away trip the does, to interbreed with strangers and dilute their gene pool. The few who don't, pass on to their offspring a gift for quiet desperation—the trait I now observe in poor hungry males among the hawthorns.

Some concrete evidence for this scenario comes from Pleistocene cave art, made by the Keen-Ears. In these paintings, herds of thorny-looking quadrupeds slant across the limestone. Following them are hominid hunters, leaning on their spears in a peculiarly pensive manner, which no one, who has seen and pitied the Pluricorn, can possibly mistake.

5

When people in my part of the world think of Truth, with a capital T, it conjures images of hands on Bibles, mathematical equations, or a pure unearthly light that pierces through all lies and obscurities. Truth is close in our imaginations to God, so we don't associate it with anything that creeps, flies, swims, or walks the earth in animal form. But personally, I wouldn't bother with the Bible if I could swear on a vampire bat.

Truth Bats

Pᴇᴏᴘʟᴇ ʀᴀʀᴇʟʏ ᴅɪsᴄᴜss how one's voice changes after telling a lie, because no one wants to admit to falsehood. I will confess, however, that I once told my sister a premeditated, consequential lie. My voice changed instantly: my small-talk became robotic, my heartfelt words sounded plagiarized, and even phrases muttered to myself had a disingenuous tone. Like everyone whose voice is deserted by the "ring of truth," I had lost my bats. We owe the ring of truth in the human voice to Truth Bats, an invisible subspecies of vampire bat, and thereby hangs (upside down) the tale of how I was inspired to write this book.

Vampire bats are a superior species, surpassing humans in their altruism and their ability to tell truth from lies. Consider: a vampire bat must feed every couple of days, or die. When a bat's hunting goes badly, though, it doesn't worry—it can turn to the luckier bats hanging with it, upside down, from a roost. The hungry bat visits each, emitting a begging call, and the others disgorge a donation of blood so their friend won't starve. But since the

savvy bats also recognize voices, they know who is begging, and if a hungry bat has not helped other bats in the
past, it is unlikely to receive charity. This is the Golden
Rule, with teeth. Who wants to regurgitate hard-earned
blood to someone who'll ignore you the next time you're
in need? And if a callous, greedy bat should die of hunger,
those genes are no loss to the species, which as a whole
benefits from generosity. Even more impressively, when
a bat lies—when it goes begging despite a full belly—by
various means, the other bats know the difference. For
Truth Bats, the key is in the voice.

It's a pity that Truth Bats are invisible, because they're
so cute—like furry plum pits with mouse ears, three-inch
wingspans, and expressions of pipsqueak ferocity. They
live in small clusters, lap the blood of nocturnal moths,
and roost, by day, on the bodies of large mammals. They
are clean, easy guests, dining and digesting elsewhere,
bringing only their need to sleep safely, and a tendency to
chatter among themselves. Like our eyelash follicle mites,
they go unnoticed. But when it comes to humans, Truth
Bats are picky: they will only adorn the hair or clothes of
a truthful person. How do they know?

When we tell a lie, our larynx muscles contract, pro-
ducing an inaudible signal sometimes used in lie detec-
tion. Truth Bats hear this signal and fear it; their small,
tight-knit society really cannot afford bloodsucking liars
in its midst, so the lie signal is a strong negative stimulus.
When it emanates from their own roost—everywhere in

their house!—they leave in a hurry. Their departure has consequences. Truth Bats chatter as they hang together, and their continuous piping makes a background to our speech that we don't hear, but feel—something like the tingling echo of a waterfall just before your ears catch it. This is the "ring of truth." When your bats depart, scattering into the air as you trot out some whopper of a lie, your voice loses its reassuring background, and people feel that. You have more trouble persuading them; you have trouble persuading yourself. Until your Truth Bats return, you feel forlorn, lonesome, awkward, and unreal. Of course, there are liars who revel in their mendacity and don't miss the bats one bit; it's a kind of deficiency. But forlorn, lonesome, awkward, and unreal was how I felt on the day I went to visit my cousin Helen, because of a lie I had told.

"Do I sound funny to you?" I demanded, looking up at Helen. She sat on her porch, spinning silk on her hi-tech spinning wheel, a compact disk the height of her knee. Helen and I are cousins many times removed, but we've always been close, as the two oddballs in a large clan of scientists: Helen went into the arts, while I, of course, am the invisible-beast spotter. For years, we've shared our peculiar ways of seeing things. Helen belongs to a world-wide fiber arts collective called the Fibettes; all around the globe, Fibettes pick sticky cocoons off trees and ship them to other Fibettes, who spin them. Through Helen's hands pass the silks of many latitudes, to become a single, fine, homespun thread. Except for the modern wheel, my cousin resembles her great-grandmother, a Chippewa-Irish farmer, with black braids down her back, a work-hardened body in a cotton shift, and patient eyes.

"You sound . . . not yourself, Sophie. What's wrong?"

I climbed the porch steps feeling wretched, though it was a lazy July afternoon, and the porch was shaded by a canopy of honeysuckle, pagoda-shaped, fragrant, and loud with floating bees.

"I'd like your advice," I said, "and I brought you something." I held out a basketful of Grand Tour cocoons. Helen stopped her treadle action, lifted her worn fingers from the thread, and took the basket, peering in. I put one of the invisible cocoons in her palm, and soon she was plucking them out by touch alone.

"Get me a bushel of these and an emperor," she smiled. "What's up?" I slumped on the steps, swiping away tears, and confessed how I had lied to my sister Evie when she unearthed an Asian honeybee from the Pleistocene epoch, mysteriously preserved in North America. Because I'd feared for the Keen-Ears' safety if their existence became generally known, I had not revealed that invisible animals turn visible in death, or that Evie's puzzling bee had come to the New World with invisible humans who still farmed its descendants for honey.

Helen listened (patiently, considering the irritating, unnatural voice in which I spoke) and spun. There was going to be a long stretch of invisibility in her thread, where the Grand Tour cocoons spun out, and I wondered what she'd use it for. In her braids' tips hung some dark, wrapped objects resembling cigars for dolls, and I envied her—artistic, enjoying life, with Truth Bats.

"I had no choice," I sniffled. "I deliberately misled Evie about those bees. What else could I do? Was I supposed to open the door to genocide? So I lied. My bats disappeared. All my life I've had Truth Bats. Now they're gone, and anything I say, like 'all my life I've had Truth Bats'— it doesn't *sound* true. It sounds like I don't know what. Helen, you know, the bats are not even comfortable with social fibs, and I've gone and told a *big* lie to my sister. That doesn't sound true either. God, I want my bats back!"

"Poor old God," Helen murmured, guiding her evolving thread. "Well. What will bring your bats back?"

"Telling Evie the truth. Until I do, my voice is polluted by deceptive stress," I explained with unnerving glibness.

"Then tell. Trust Evie. Don't you trust your sister?"

"She has an obligation to science." Helen tut-tutted as if the ambiguous ethics of scientific research were a minor tangle in her skein. Her voice, I noted wistfully, was mild, full, and wholesome as sweetgrass.

"Sophie, in your shoes, I would figure it this way. I would rather get back my bats, and have Evie find out about the Keen-Ears, than live with a lie and wait for some unknown person to discover them. You know it will come. You can't hide a natural fact." She licked her thumbs to feel the invisible thread as it passed through them. I threw back my head, inhaled the honeysuckle scent, and shut my eyes. After a while, the purr of the spinning wheel paused and Helen said, "Why don't you go down to the barn and call her now?"

AFTER I'D CALLED EVIE from Helen's barn, I ran up the porch steps, and my cousin rose to hug me. My joints were trembling as if I'd dropped a loaded barbell, but I had no time to linger. My sister, grasping only that I had urgent business, had said to drop by now, while she had an opportune moment. Helen wished me good luck. As I drove into town and hunted for a parking space around Evie's campus, I rehearsed aloud phrases of apology and ethical pleas, all of which sounded like excuses and false promises; they left me feeling vaguely felonious as I trotted down the corridors of the Life Science Center, through the noise mix of freezers and centrifuges, past office doors, laboratories, and the absentminded or cordial faces of Evie's colleagues and students. I found Evie in a small workroom adjacent to her main lab.

"Come in," she said. "Let's talk while I feed the Worm."

Entering, my nostrils contracted. The dim room smelled of mold, with substenches that evoked thoughts of continents passing through the guts of earthworms. Around the walls, floor to ceiling, ran shiny brown tubing like a coiled snakeskin: this was the Worm. If you uncoiled it, you'd have a torus—a donut-shaped tube filled with silts, clays, sands, loams, and small wildlife: bacteria, fungi, nematodes. The Worm helped Evie to experiment with soil gases. Its "skin" was her invention, a polymer sheath containing molecular valves and electronic sensors. As soil gases within hit the valves, thumbtack-sized "scales" covering the Worm changed attitude, like ailerons, so that segments of it bristled or lay smooth, in recognizable patterns. Meanwhile, the sensors, through remote pickups, fed blooms of data into a digital console, where my sister sat dangling her short legs from an ergonomic stool. In the artificial twilight, Evie's white lab coat was an eerie noncolor that reached behind my eyes. Wielding an automatic pipette, she squirted ingredients through a filtering lid into a large glass retort filled with nutrient slurry.

"Evie," I declared, "I have an apology to make, and an explanation."

"Oh?" said Evie. "Shoot." While I had my say (sounding much like an inflight announcement of unavoidable delays) she completed her mixture, discarded the filter, screwed the lid tighter on the retort, and set it on a magnetic stirrer. The slurry began to form a sluggish vortex, and the magnet at the retort's bottom, unseen, made repetitive whacking sounds. After I'd finished talking, Evie turned to me with a bright smile of affection.

"No problem, I'm glad you told me all this. You're sweet."

For a few moments, I watched my sister's precise

movements as she checked the output of dials and LED displays. Then I asked, "What are you going to do with the information I just gave you?" (The question had a distinct soap-opera tone.)

"Nothing," Evie said.

My thoughts were, to put it mildly, in disarray. I should have been relieved that the first impulse of Evie, and through her, science, was not to spring with full force upon the Keen-Ears ... Yet, riffling mentally through the images that had driven me to lie—slain Keen-Ears roped to hunters' trucks, caged Keen-Ears in military labs, their bees scattered in dying colonies—I felt, instead of relief, shock; and as it passed, hopelessness. Ironically enough, my life was premised on the belief that science would someday take over the study of invisible animals. I'd always assumed that this transition would happen, in a vague green future. It had to happen, that was the premise. Someday, somehow, nations would be wiser, and invisible animals would be studied. But if Evie thought nothing of my information—*nothing*—where did that leave my work and the meaning of my life?

"But," I said, in a tone so strange that my sister stopped her activities and drew her sandy brows together.

"But what." Evie's emotions were simple, like four colored stripes: warmth, self-regard, impatience, and curiosity. Right now I was seeing the middle two in her eyes, like half a plaid.

"I gave you the key to researching invisible animals," I

said. "It doesn't seem to have registered. Do you think I'm telling fairy tales?"

"Oh, come *on*." One stripe, impatience, glinting. "I don't deserve this. When did I call ever them 'fairy tales'? When did I *ever* not make time to talk with you and give you information?"

I rubbed my face, in a sad muddle. Evie was right— whether from our family tradition of tolerance toward the invisible-beast spotter, or sisterly affection, or both, she had always given me her best professional guesses about invisible beasts. She spoke sincerely, I knew, because in her coat pocket's corner, beside a pair of latex gloves, hung four Truth Bats who must have felt exactly like balls of lint. I apologized again, this time for having doubted her open-mindedness, and my sister—the gold stripe of warmth flashing from her hazel eyes—told me to forget it, shaking her bangs (impatiently) as I made to rise.

"Sit down, sit! I never see you, Soph. You could be invisible yourself." I obeyed. My sister tore the wrapper from a sterile nozzle, twisted it into the retort's lid, popped the nozzle into the pump that supplied the Worm, and began pouring in nutrient slurry. Her students had decorated the Worm's pump to resemble the dragon's head in a Chinese New Year parade; its red tongue lolled at Evie, tipping slurry down its throat, like the Hound of the Baskervilles being shown a T-bone steak.

"Suppose," I resumed painfully, "suppose I were to trap some invisible bees and bring them here? What would happen?" Evie unhooked the emptied retort, smiling, her four feelings prettily displayed together.

"Okay—so, like, your invisible bees build a beehive in my office and sting my students. What does that prove?" Evie answered herself. "It proves nothing. Scientists study a huge amount of phenomena that we don't directly see. Like soil gases." She nodded at the Worm, its scales rippling from its lunch. "There are theories that explain what soil gases are, and predict their effects. I work with those theories. If I find the right effects and my work is reproducible—great, I get an article in *Science*. Here's the long answer to your question, Soph. There isn't any theory that explains, or predicts, like, invisible bees. If I tried to work on that problem, I'd be a joke. People would totally start calling my lab, like, 'Ghostbusters Lab' and 'Uri Geller Lab,' and my career would be trashed. I'm not saying your invisibles don't exist. Just, nobody's going to touch them. The Keen-Ears are safe! Isn't that what you want?" She cocked her head. Then a deep, reverberant, bass belch boomed out of the Worm's speakers, and I gave a startled cry.

"My students," said Evie, faintly embarrassed. "They program the Worm's sound. They call it 'Smaug.'"

THE DAY AFTER I'D TALKED to Evie, it rained. I visited Helen in her studio, a barn scented with lanolin from racks of yarn. Baskets dangled from the rafters, containing everything from Japanese ribbons to stacks of felt. Her worktables were crowded with Swiss sewing computers. The kettle was whistling in a corner, and I made mint tea, waiting for Helen to emerge from her partitioned-off "loom room." The racket from the loom room drowned out the hush of rain. Helen came out, saw me, and arched her back; then she spilled forward to rest her palms and braids on the floor. The backs of weavers always hurt. She rolled her spine straight again with care. We took our teacups and sat on pillows beside a work-in-progress spread on the floor; at first glance, it looked like the reverse side of a scatter rug. Bending closer, I drew an awed breath. Hundreds of small knots formed the fabric, each knot embroidered with an individual face: a yawning baby, a thoughtful old man, a laughing schoolgirl, a glamorous rapper, a tired workman in a blue cap, a worried woman with an eye patch . . . I wanted to lie down on it and join my intractable story to all the others.

"I thought you'd ask, 'Where are the animals?'" Helen said. "Then I was going to say, 'They're invisible.'" I gazed at her, speechless. "How are your Truth Bats? What? Oh, no."

I folded my arms on my knees, dropped my head, and began nodding in despair. "Don't do that," Helen admonished. "You have to think. I'll help you. Try to remember what you said, and what your sister said." I related my conversation with Evie, ears cringing from the false tone of my voice. "Huh," Helen murmured. "That's interesting."

"I'm glad you think so." Even my bitchiness sounded canned. Helen stretched out her right hand and pulled back on it with her left, wincing; then she repeated the stretch on her left hand.

"Isn't that what you want?" she asked. "For the Keen-Ears to be left alone? Why are you let down?"

"Because my bats are still gone. I told Evie the whole truth, and my bats are still gone. I've done everything I can." I sounded like an ad for a weight-loss drug. "I've done everything I can!" Now it was an antidepressant.

"You keep saying that," Helen pointed out, blowing steam off her tea. "Maybe that's what they don't like. Are you sure you've done everything you can, to tell the truth about your invisible animals?" I thought hard, while the rainy wind outside disturbed a shingle.

"What more can I do? I gave a biologist the key to it all. I'm not a scientist."

Helen glanced up, and her eyes were cold water over granite. Still cradling her cup in both hands, she unfolded her legs, rose in one movement, and walked away across the barn. I scrambled up and followed. Helen stopped by a worktable, lifted a strip of transparent chiffon, and let it hang quivering as the air nudged it. It was long, trailing over the other side of the table and onto the floor.

"These are digital lists of the names of soldiers who have been killed in the war," she said. Looking closer, I saw faint gray lines and characters—printouts of a Web site, names afloat like ghosts. "The idea came from

Victorian mourning handkerchiefs, and it's turning into an installation. I'm not the president," Helen continued. "I can't order the war to stop. I'm not in Congress. But I can do this. Here, you look."

Helen walked off to the loom room. I understood her message: do what you can do. But what could I do? I stood holding her impalpable memorial on my palms, the names of dead young people sliding across one another; the chiffon whispered. Its whisper brought something back to me. It was the way I'd wake in the morning. When that first, fresh ray peeled off the sun and struck my bed, I'd sit up, so grateful to be delivered from fogs of dreams, and toss back my hair, feeling for the little soft pendants, humming like batteries, threading the air of a new day with inaudible vibrations, unheard pings and pips and pipings . . . that was what I missed most. My bats didn't know me, as I thought of "me." But I loved them—those winged, voracious, still small voices who unfailingly returned out of the night, as long as I didn't fail them. Without them, I was less than myself, cut off. The sound of falsehood in my voice was the sound of disconnection from my fellow creatures. If I loved Truth Bats, it was because they restored me to the authentic weave of being; and how many amateur naturalists like me, in thrall to that connected feeling—bird-watchers, shell collectors, fanciers of mosses, rockhounds, star-gazers—had faithfully recorded the odd facts that scientists eventually (when theories allowed) undertook to explain? The love of truth was an animal feeling. For its sake, I must not fail my Truth Bats.

Laying down my cousin's work carefully, I paced to the back of the barn, where a dressmaker's mannequin stood before a three-sided mirror. The stuffed torso was unadorned and full of pins and chalk marks.

"Helen," I called, "you've given me an idea! For something else I can try." Now, despite every effort to recall this episode, I can't remember how my voice sounded when I called out those words. I was so taken by the idea of a book about invisible beasts that I failed to notice. What I do remember is that I glanced automatically at myself in the mirror, then came closer to inspect my hair.

Like a cluster of black grapes in the tresses of a bacchante, a flock of Truth Bats hung from my crown to my shoulder. With catkin bodies and jet-pointed wings, they made a voluptuous, yet dainty, headdress. I heard a baby bat shrilling for its mother, a sound as fine as a beading needle passing through the eye of a sewing needle. Helen came up behind me in the mirror. Guessing the news immediately from my expression, she grinned and unrolled a length of cloth.

"See what I made with your invisible thread. Isn't it nice?"

And in truth, it was.

6

---

*C*ities are growing all the time, and animals evolve with them. Rats chew through lead and cement; songbirds add the sounds of car alarms and construction equipment to their repertoires. Cliff swallows are evolving shorter wings for faster takeoffs from roadways to their nests in overpasses. The evolution of urban nonhumans is so closely tied to our habits that it may yet overturn Gertrude Stein's famous dictum, "The thing that differentiates man from animals is money." The Wild Rubber Jack has evolved for the urban niche of business districts. He may not have a credit rating yet, but he follows the money.

The Wild Rubber Jack

THE WILD RUBBER JACK is commonly found in cities and likes to keep company with humans, having a sociable nature. The Jack (for brevity's sake) is an invisible American ass. It is, in fact, an invisible offshoot of the revolutionary breed that George Washington created in this country, with the aid of the famous stud "King of Malta," a gift of the Marquis de Lafayette, at a time when our nation's development depended on the hard work of powerful jackasses. Thanks to Washington's improvements, American Mammoth Jacks can stand as tall as a man. To this day, we lead the world in the enormous size of our asses.

The Wild Rubber Jack, though in every other way a perfect ass—with his wise, gentle eyes, cream velvet nose, and patient demeanor—carries no burdens. It would not be smart to try and ride him. (I use the male pronoun here for the same reason, whatever it might be, that the breed called Mammoth Jack is not called Mammoth Jenny.)

His joints are the distinguishing characteristic of the

Jack: in them, nature displays one of her oddest combinations, giving a mammal the advantages of an insect. Grasshoppers, fleas, mosquitoes, and other insects possess a material in their joints that zoologists call "animal rubber." Its real name is *resilin*, a very stretchy and elastic protein. Resilin allows fleas to make prodigious jumps—like having bungee cords in your joints. It allows locusts to save a third of the energy of the wing downstroke for the upstroke, and mosquitoes to expand their abdomens for a large meal, then return to a smaller size. The Wild Rubber Jack has resilin in his croup, hocks, and fetlocks, allowing him to kick much farther than the ordinary ass. Thanks to his rubberized hindquarters, the Jack can kick out his heels some eight to ten feet from where he stands, in an arc of 180 degrees, and keep kicking as long as he feels the need to. The hindquarters of a Wild Rubber Jack are like an invisible cross between Elastic Man and Bruce Lee.

His favorite haunts are among lunching executives, oblivious to their pockets and handbags, in which he grazes for antacids, breath mints, tobacco, nicotine gum, diet candy, and raw almonds in Ziploc bags. That's why, at lunchtime, the Jack becomes a social menace. If one party makes a deal-breaking remark and the other party sits up abruptly, chafing the Jack's sensitive nose in a trouser pocket, or displacing it from a handbag, the Jack reacts with a back-kick that causes choking, turning purple, and the somersaulting of forks. Worse, and not infrequently, the Jack causes cardiac failure among workers who rush along corridors carrying lunch back to their desks. Drawn to the smell of food in their sacks, and exasperated by their speed, the Jack lashes out at their chests just to slow them down, and succeeds only too well. It's important not to blame the animal, but to remember that his skittish responses are the heritage of all wild creatures that depend on the global business environment.

Neither my profession nor my tax bracket brings me into the Jack's company very often, but one Jack did make a bad date memorable. I will never forget being taken to dinner by a corporate lawyer who confided, over the white truffle–truffled breast of ruffed grouse, his thoughts on the legal concept of damages.

"All relationships can be translated into money, Sophie," he said. "This is America." This made me so sad that I desperately signaled the waiter for the dessert menu, and in doing so jostled a soft palpitant donkey nose with my elbow, and the next thing I knew, there was shiraz on everything, and I never heard from him again.

In the Book of Numbers, a famous ass, a jenny, is beaten by the prophet Balaam because she refuses to trot forward. She sees an angel with a flaming sword barring her way, and being a sensible beast, she balks, then sidles against a brick wall, crushing Balaam's foot, then lies down under the incensed prophet, who has been oppressing her all the while with blows and insults. At this point, two miracles happen. The first is that the jenny speaks to Balaam, asking him if he hasn't noticed anything unusual. The second is that Balaam, the human, actually pays attention to her. When he does, he too sees the avenging angel. And duly apologizes. How does this story relate to the Wild Rubber Jack? Well, according to Scripture, angels with fiery swords guard the Garden of Eden to keep humanity from creeping back in and parking our trailers. Viewed in that light, the story means that we should accept the inevitable: Eden is closed. The good times are over. Suck it in. Bust your butt. Sweat till you drop. Forward, march! This message of humility in the face of the inevitable, or divine will, or creative destruction, or whatever it cares to call itself, is aptly delivered by a humble ass of the visible sort, used to taking orders and being ridden and beaten.

The invisible ass is another story entirely. If Balaam had laid a finger on the Wild Rubber Jack, that beast would have gone nose to the dirt and flipped the prophet like a flapjack onto the angel's head, then gone off to crop a thistle. The Wild Rubber Jack takes no abuse, not even from the person with the carrots (or almonds). Unlike Balaam's ass, however, he does not talk. His voice isn't known for good advice. It's only the same outrageous, hilarious, earsplitting bray that wild asses have evolved, over the millennia, to call to each other across the untamed deserts and solitudes.

7

Thousands of years before humans began domesticating livestock, wolves domesticated humans. Enjoying our garbage heaps, wolves who were bold and friendly set out to make us share the warm, safe spots at our firesides where cooking went on, and the choicest scraps were to be had. They learned our body language better than any other nonhuman species, dogging our every move—and they became dogs. Since then, we have evolved in intimate mutuality. Anyone who thinks that dogs are mere servile pets may learn from the following tale how our consciousness is controlled by those whom we think we have mastered.

The Riddle of Invisible Dogs

At the time of this tale I was, you might say, between dogs. Because I can't live without a dog, whenever I lose one of these companions whose only unforgiveable fault is growing old so fast, it's just a matter of time until a new dog arrives to lick the bowls of a beloved predecessor. Meanwhile, I volunteer at the Humane Society, where my dogs come from. This time, my duties consisted of riding once a week with Lucas, a retired policeman who worked as a humane officer, to enforce the anticruelty laws. We rode in a van with cages in the back and a sheaf of that day's abuse reports on the dashboard. Most were cases of neglect, and the more I saw, the more I thought about neglect, until I made the discovery recounted here.

Lucas had heavy-lidded eyes, a self-contained manner, and the build of a sea lion. Filling the doorways of rich and poor alike, of dilapidated row houses and pseudo-Tudor "manors," he politely pointed out the facts. *Sir, maybe you don't take the dog inside enough, because his belly is all hard mud and I see this hole he dug to get out*

*of the rain . . . Sir, your dog needs veterinary attention, the
chain is growing into her neck and the skin is infected, see?
. . . Ma'am, the dogs were locked in the house you left, maybe
you didn't notice but it's not the realtor's responsibility . . .
Ma'am, your son has the right to play paintball, but for the
dog's fur to look like this, and shaking like this, it's not good
for the animal, no?*

We'd ride around all morning. At lunchtime, we'd
park outside a donut shop, get coffee, and eat in the van,
where Lucas would open his insulated cooler for the
stash of steamed tamales his wife made every day. Since
he insisted on sharing them, I began bringing home-
made fudge. We both licked our fingertips. Briefly, the
van lit up with gold and green summery scents of maize
and moist corn husks, and in a convivial interlude, the
gray scenes of neglect would fade. Then we'd get back
on the road, often returning to the Society with con-
fiscated animals. I would wonder if the time had come
to bring home one of the rescued pooches. When Dog
Day finally arrived, however, it was not at all what I had
anticipated.

Lucas and I rode to a suburban household that had
been reported by its neighbors many times before. We
parked beside a rise, topped by a modest house overlooking a flight of limestone steps appropriate for a museum,
and, to one side, a stone cloister with lancet arches. We
climbed to the front door, rang, and waited. Below, the
cloister disclosed to our view not the swimming pool I

expected, but a giant plaster crocodile and two tall, grappling plaster pandas.

"You can tell he's *un poco loco*," Lucas said. We exchanged a look. The door cracked open, and Lucas asked a nose-tip and lips for the name of the dog owner.

"I dunno," said the lips.

"We're taking the dog, it's really skinny."

"Okay, you take the dog, it's not my dog."

"Someone is needed to sign, to surrender it."

The door slammed. We went back down the steps into a yard in which stood a pavilion tent, with scalloped trim, near a flailing black-and-gray banner staked to the ground. The black stripes flashed, the gray stripes shimmered, and walking over to this heraldic vision, we found a German shepherd so thin she was almost two-dimensional—the dark stripes were shadows between her bones. Lucas took a cell phone picture. Then he lassoed the dog's head with a nylon lead, untied her, and hauled her—sniffing and nibbling his pants for biscuits—into the back of the van. She cried as we drove away.

"I love cases like this one," Lucas confided. "The evidence is right there. One photo in court. I take the dog and go." We rode underneath the city zoo's footbridge painted with multicolored beasts, all grinning like humans.

"So," I said, "I looked up the word *neglect* in the dictionary. It comes from a Latin word, *lego*. Guess what that means?"

"'Lego'? It sounds like you're talking to a big dog bitin' on your leg."

"It means 'to choose' and 'to read.' Two different things. I'm wondering, what do those things have in common?" My companion looked sleepy, thinking it over.

"Paying attention," he said.

"Ha! So . . . the real meaning of neglecting a dog is, not paying attention?"

"*No prestan atencion*," Lucas agreed, in the Spanish of sound generalizations. "This guy," he thumbed backward, "he's already got so many charges—animal cruelty is nothing. He neglects the dog because he can always get another one. And I'll have to go and rescue it again."

When I came home, I lit a fire in my den and sat before it on the hearth bricks. It was October, a good season for contemplation. The walls and ceiling pulsed with ruddy tints. In the bay window, above the woods outside, in a mist of bluish clouds, rose a fiery moon. I drank a glass of wine, made a plateful of bleu cheese on crackers, and heard coyotes yipping to bring the pack together for the night's hunt—cheery, eerie, noisy coyotes, the free canids of the earth, the ones who scorned pethood. Did they have a better evolutionary deal than dogs? I thought about the gray wolves that once lived in my woods; wolves might have denned where I sat now, with their big heads and icy eyes. And I thought about the young bitch we'd just rescued. Tonight, at least, she was better off than most coyotes: she slept beside a tray filled with more kibble than she could eat. This overfull tray would stay in her cage till she relaxed enough to allow others around her food, without attacking. Then would I be ready to adopt her?

I reached for my cheese crackers—and they weren't there. Absentmindedly, I'd brought an empty plate to the fireside . . . I went back to the kitchen, made cheese crackers, and returned.

The fire, still in its yellow youth, rushed from a bed of breathing embers. I revisited the memory of my last dog, also a German shepherd. Her eyes were intense and sweet, like espresso, and she pushed limits. Forbidden to put her paws on the bed, she'd jump up and put her elbows on the bed instead, her paws scrupulously curled in the air. She had hated closed doors. Every door in the house had been nudged ajar by a slim nose, snuffling through flared nostrils, like a black space probe from a planet of fur . . . I missed a hundred special things about her. Now she was gone out of the universe. How, I wondered, how could anyone live with a dog and *not* pay attention?

I reached for my cheese crackers, and they weren't there. Shaking my buzzed head, I thought I must have eaten them without noticing—shame on me, not paying attention!—and went back to the kitchen to make more, and returned.

By now, my fire had aged to pink cubes, architecturally

heaped, under blue flames chasing their tails. Suddenly, in the darkness, the den shook to a loud thud—my farmer neighbor's twelve-gauge shotgun, aimed at the coyotes. Then the farmer's corgis barked telegraphically across fields and woods, and some Great Pyrenees, from a nearby sheepfold, uttered deep grunts, as if to say, "Uh-huh, we hear you." These sounds had the aspect of a question put as directly as possible. Which was the better evolutionary deal for canids—freedom and the farmer's shotgun, or pethood and neglect? All the pitiable horrors I'd witnessed streamed through my wine-weakened mind, all the sadness I'd thought I'd gotten used to. Needing comfort, I reached for my cheese crackers.

They weren't there. Again.

"This is getting monotonous!" I yelled aloud. Then I saw, on the softly pulsing wall, the shadow of a wolf.

I looked around and caught a German shepherd—a big tan brute with ears like trowels—in the act of using my sofa for a dinner napkin, running his muzzle along the cushions and back the other way.

"Bad doggie," I said, with feeling. "Bad!" He startled: his ears wilted, his sandy tail melded to his white belly, and he skulked into the kitchen, where, darting at me looks of shock and awe, he trotted into the gap between the sink and the stove, as far as his shoulders, and drooped his head against the wall. He huddled there, rib cage pumping, panting and yawning with stress. A whiff of dog sweat filled the air. What had I done?

What happened next was predictable. I spent the rest of the evening cooking for a dog. I spent the rest of the year training my new dog. I named him Wolf, for wolfing my snacks. And I discovered that he was invisible.

MY DISCOVERY BEGAN when the postal carrier slid out of her car with a packet in hand, and walked straight into a dog sniffing her sneakers. As I opened my mouth to call him, she stepped forward, and kept stepping, exactly where Wolf was not. I stared openmouthed, missing my cue about the nice sunshine we were having.

"I'm so sorry, he isn't trained yet," I said. She looked puzzled. "The dog," I added. "He's new."

"You got a dog? I'm glad he's not out, I hate it when dogs get out." She smiled, getting back into the car as Wolf tried to goose her.

Then Mike, of Mike's Raccoon Wranglers, came to install shields in my chimney. Wolf trotted out, tongue shaking like a long jelly, straight toward the braced, separated knees of an unsuspecting Mike, who surveyed my roof . . . and sidestepped, boots suddenly nimble. He unfolded his ladder with the motions, if not the conversation, of a workman avoiding a large dog.

"Sorry about the dog," I said. Mike looked puzzled. "See the dog?" I asked. Still holding the ladder, with a slightly defensive air, Mike looked all around me. "Oh! Never mind," I apologized rapidly, "I thought I saw—the

neighbor's dog out there, in the yard, but it was only—
oh! Never mind, I must have seen the woodchuck." Mike
laughed and climbed the ladder. All the while, Wolf
stood leaning on my legs, panting with pleasure. Conclusions framed themselves. But I knew invisible animals, and I knew people, and this was not the proper
behavior of people around invisible animals. They should
not be avoiding what they could not see.

All my life I had known that there were plenty of
invisible dogs around; now I faced the surprising fact
that I'd never thought seriously about them. I had
known that among the unleashed dogs passing me in the
street, sniffing behind bushes, or posting liquid messages
on trees, a goodly number were not visible to normal
humans—but somehow, this had never provoked either
wonder, or basic questions. I hadn't paid attention! Perhaps the fault lay with my childhood bedtime stories,
which were often about an invisible poodle named Tidbit, who had shyly but persistently dogged Granduncle
Erasmus on his extensive travels through Europe, Africa,
and what he'd called "the Orient." At the bottom of my
mind, all invisible dogs were Tidbit, whom I had out-
grown, and about whom I had no more questions than
I did about swing sets. Shame on me, because the basic
questions were burning ones—and Granduncle Erasmus
was no longer here to answer them.

Fortunately, a rich cousin of mine (who wishes to remain anonymous) funds and administers a private archive of my family's records. I visited this chilled, silent repository, and delved deeply into the papers of the invisible-beast spotters who had preceded me in our genealogy. I read till my eyes watered, taking notes. The papers went back centuries; the oldest ones, too fragile for handling, had to be viewed online. Not one of those diaries, legal documents, scholarly articles, newspapers, handbills, scrapbooks, broadsides, or letters (the most plentiful item) explained why people avoided a dog they could not see. On the other hand, I gathered a good deal of interesting information, and was able to piece together a partial portrait of invisible dogs; I call them Invies, for short.

The most suggestive item was that Invies seemed to arrive in normal litters; I found no mention of their breeding true. A recessive trait, perhaps? Equal in interest was the fact that they were scavengers, lurking around dumps and households, in a gray area between wildness and domesticity. And they were quite timid. An Elizabethan ancestor—an irascible barber-surgeon who'd lived with a pack of invisible sheepdogs—described them succinctly as *Cringeing Curs, tho Artful and eke Thievish.* On rare occasions, Invies had formed attachments to my family's invisible-beast spotters. Tidbit, for instance, would not allow herself to be petted, yet had followed my grand-uncle around the world. Likewise, a nineteenth-century ancestress—an Ohio schoolmistress who had written a prizewinning monograph on edible cattails—had lived on warm terms with an Invie collie named Hecuba. Recording her cattail honors, this lady wrote in her diary, *Hecuba being so very spoilt, I cannot but reflect how easy a thing it is for that much nearer invisible companion, my Soul, to be as spoilt by worldly Vanities.* Helpfully, this diary also described Hecuba's behavior in the litter where she'd been discovered. The details accorded with other hints about the puppyhood of Invies. They were, in the canine social hierarchy, lower than the lowest— virtual outcasts, not assertive at all: if their littermates merely inhaled with the intention of growling, the little Invies rolled over and piddled on themselves. In adult life, Invies' groveling status and habits gave them advantages. My granduncle had seen Tidbit snatch scraps from under the nose of a bullmastiff, who had given her a glare instead of a shredded ear. These instances, I noted, must mean that visible animals could see invisible dogs—an idea that violated one of my first principles, namely, that only invisible animals could see other invisible animals. An exception to this rule was hard to credit. Yet, if I accepted the anecdotes, it seemed that an Invie's subsocial status canceled dogs' usual responses, giving it a few precious, life-preserving privileges, similar to the position of the fool in a medieval court. And like fools, Invies were highly intelligent; it went with the territory.

I LEARNED MUCH FROM the archives, but not what I came for. Why did people avoid a dog that they could not see? The question remained unanswered. A last-resort possibility was, simply, that Wolf *wasn't* invisible. After all, I reasoned, a postal carrier and a raccoon wrangler were not a reliable sample. To test Wolf's invisibility, I should bring him out in public, among lots of random people. I put on a dress with long drippy sleeves, slipped a tote bag over my arm, and secured Wolf by a leash tucked behind my sleeves and the bag. Thus attired, I went with my dog to the hairdresser.

Nobody noticed at first. The lavender-haired sylphs behind the register greeted me with their usual sweetness. The businesswomen sipped their imported water with lemon slices, imperturbably, at the bar. The old wives who had almost stopped caring, who were here for an hour's vacation, maternally told their stylists that their hair looked very nice. A row of plastic-draped ladies being shampooed in dark marble sinks, their bare feet elevated on chair rests, did not so much as twitch their freshly lacquered toes when those toes exerted a strong fascination on Wolf, whom I had to drag back by his camouflaged leash. Nobody looked twice. My hairdresser, pinning a cape around my neck as I nestled in her padded chair—with Wolf huddled under her counter, violently sneezing—proceeded to step over his paws, and, as he grew bolder, to dodge his slinking forays around her cart. When he retired again underneath the counter, he assumed such obscurity, such utter unnoticedness, that I almost forgot he was there. My point was proved, I thought.

Then someone saw him.

The witness lay on a settee by the manicurist's station, to the right of my chair. It was a turquoise suede coat. Abruptly, one of its sleeves jerked forward, while the rest of the coat slewed helplessly, flashing its satin lining.

"No, no!" shouted the coat's owner, her nails still spread before the eyebrow-hiked manicurist. "Fluffy! Bad girl!" The sleeve, with earsplitting cries, extruded part of a Bichon Frisé, a sort of bubble bath with a nose, who pumped her lamblike forelegs up and down with great vigor, prevented from shooting forth by a sparkly collar. "What's gotten into her—I'm so *sorry*," gasped her owner, untying a turquoise leash, "I'll take her to the car—*excuse* me—"

Everyone stared at Fluffy, carried off in frothing disgrace. No one looked at me except my hairdresser, who made a disparaging remark.

"Little yappy dogs, the way they go off about nothing," she said. I glanced at Wolf, who could have, if he'd wished, inhaled Fluffy. He was glued to the floor, quaking in terror.

MY EXPERIMENT AT THE HAIRDRESSER'S raised more questions than it answered. Why, why did people avoid a dog they could not see? And now that I'd seen the incredible departure from the rule—why did visible animals see an invisible dog? Why did Fluffy, and the bullmastiff who had glared at Tidbit, and the Invies' littermates, see what humans did not? These questions made my head ache. It was time to call Evie for advice. I picked up the phone and told her all about it.

"Evie," I entreated, "is there a way that humans can see something, but not be conscious that they do?"

"Oh sure! There's a documented phenomenon called 'inattentional blindness.' In the classic study, they made college students watch a film of a basketball game and count the bounce shots. A woman in a gorilla suit walked onto the court, in the middle of the game, beat her chest—I love that part—and walked off. So, like, only four percent of the students who saw the film noticed the gorilla, which is totally what my students would do. Does that help?"

"Maybe . . . but the people who didn't see my dog also stepped out of his way."

"Uh. Just a minute." I heard a young voice, a student; Evie was talking from her lab. "Yeah, uh . . . actually, that sounds like brain damage. Like people whose vision input doesn't process normally, so they're technically blind, but they navigate around things."

"I'd have to assume that everyone in the salon was

brain damaged. And what about the other dog that saw my dog?" I waited, while the student's whine rose in pitch to a pure primate screech.

"Uh ... Sophie ... think strategies, okay? It's like, they mate with other dogs, that's a reproductive strategy, but they steal from humans, that's a survival strategy, okay? Gotta go."

"Thanksandgoodluck!" I rattled as the cell phone went dead. On a sheet of paper, I scribbled the words *inattentional blindness*.

WINTER CAME. My original question stayed unanswered. I continued riding out with Lucas. Winter near the Canadian border is a fearful time for dogs whose owners aren't paying attention. Sometimes at night, I dreamed that the city turned upside down like a chandelier, from whose snow-grimed, crystal-coated chains hung, frozen alive, dogs by the hundreds, creaking as they swayed. The city police visited the Society to inspect the bodies of three spaniels who'd been nicknamed "the dogs of Christmas," whom I don't want to remember. Maybe Evie had a point: maybe the human race was brain damaged. My home in the woods, in this season, provided a respite from scenes of neglect and moral abjection. The gelid January sunshine shone brightly there, from snowstorm to snowstorm, and in the drifts I saw necklaces of coyote tracks, circling toward rusty smudges where rabbits had uttered their last screams. Those circular tracks were the pattern of hunting wolves, I knew—coyotes were also called "prairie wolves"—it was the behavior on which shepherd dogs' training was based. Outside my home, two evolutionary paths showed as distinct as black and white: pethood versus wildness. Inside my home, the path was not so clear. What was Wolf, the invisible shepherd? Science, in the form of my brilliant sister, was not helping.

But I was willing to wait for answers; after all, hadn't time been on my side where my Wolfie was concerned? We'd come a long way. I had trained him in basic obedience. And he had trained me, revealing a most un-Invie-like fondness for massage. He would fix on me a spangled brown gaze, and in a very eloquent way, fold his ears to expose the petting surface between them. If I didn't respond, he would thrust his head into my hand, to stimulate it, exploiting a human impulse straight out of some painted cavern in my brain. Whenever I took the time to massage his whole spine, skull to tail, I surfaced from that drenching in animal softness, in likeness and alienness, with the giddy rush that is our vascular reward for petting a dog; the lowered blood pressure that is the upshot of thirty thousand years of mutual evolution. My heart would open down to its molecules. So we shaped each other, and were satisfied. Now, when I lit my fire and sat before it, my dog knew better than to steal my crackers. He took them from my hand and placed each cracker on the floor, to lick it, nudge it, give it some thought. Like his human, he had a contemplative personality. When he finished eating, a wolf's shadow rippled through the firelight on the wall. Then my dog laid his head on my knee, curled his tail around my other knee, and deposited all his paws in my lap, as if for safekeeping. I ran a finger up his nose, and he shut his eyes. Whatever this invisible dog was, we were family. We were a pack.

ONE WET SPRING MORNING, outside my house, a loud horn honked. A brown UPS truck was parked, the driver's cap at a strange, stiff tilt.

"Ma'am!" he shouted. "I can't come down with that attack dog loose."

"What? What?" As I stepped out, the rest of his words got scrambled in a gust of raindrops and an almighty din, a forceful, ground-ringing noise. An animal was performing a dance in the wet pollen on the driveway, a ferocious, leaping—it was—my God! My dog. He was a vision of tawny muscles and flashing teeth. He sounded like all German shepherds: his bark was law, authorized at state and federal levels. WOOF. My invisible shepherd was visible. And I'd never taught him "heel."

"Wolf! Sit!" He paused long enough to throw me an incredulous look—"Sit," in this crisis? The UPS guy blenched, handed me my package, and backed his truck off, with gingerly twists of his tires, followed by the reverberations that Wolf found necessary to add.

"Good boy," I said, finally. Wolf became a sphere of

coarse mist. Then, with a proud grin, he licked my hand and trotted into the hostas. I was laughing. I sat down on the porch step, smacked the soggy oak pollen, and yelped with laughter. The riddle of the past year was finally answered, and like all good riddles, its answer was ridiculously obvious.

The invisible dogs were pessimists, the cynics of dogdom. They had no faith in pethood. For millennia, as long as dogs and people had shaped each other's natures, the Invies had trained us. They trained us to disregard them while they scavenged in our homes. Our eyes registered their presence, our unconscious minds took note; still, we ignored them. Good animal trainers that they were, just as we had refined wolves' natural hunting patterns, *so the Invies had refined our natural penchant for inattentional blindness.* For every yard dog licking its frozen chain with a torn tongue, or gasping away hours in the beating sun, an Invie lived in comfort through having trained a human to overlook its very existence. Obediently, we neglected them: we did not pay attention. They knew us better than we knew ourselves.

But Wolf was the exception! He had stopped being invisible because he much preferred massage. He regarded me as a uniquely valuable pack member, well worth protecting against UPS and like carriers, and had cheerfully restored himself to human sight! To reverse millennia of blindness, all it took was a little attention, a little for Christ's sake love and attention . . .

I sat grinning in the drizzle. I'd been a fool not to see it before. Now that I saw, I was still a fool, thoroughly a fool—the sort you find in the Tarot deck, a vagabond in cap and bells who strides along blindfolded, without stumbling, because he sees through the eyes of the happy dog bounding by his side.

8

I n the human body, there are ten times more bacterial cells *than human cells. Your body is a wilderness that bacteria colonize and tame. This does not diminish us—quite the contrary, it magnifies us to the dimensions of biomes; and perhaps the key to understanding ourselves as animals among other species is to be able to see the meanings of our lives in such unfamiliar, though accurate, proportions. Air Liners reveal a magnificent portrait of our human selves painted with the pointillistic brush of bacteria.*

Air Liners

To appreciate Air Liners you want to be in a bedroom at an intimate moment, and if you can observe invisible creatures, you'll see an amazing display.

You'll see something like a greenish-blue, translucent, spherical sculpture, composed of tangled legs, elbows, knees, rising and falling trunks, hands shuttling everywhere on long arms, fanning hair, arched necks, curled feet, and glinting rows of teeth. Although made by only one couple, the sphere is crowded with lots of faces—sprouting from a shoulder, lined up in rows down a flank, or staring out of a buttock, blurring from one intense expression into another, eyes popping open, sparkling, melting, or fiercely shut. The limbs and members of the sphere look hollow, and the blue-green light seems to shape them out of the air, glowing and fading. Erotic acts in which the bodies join happen in visual overlaps, so that the fingers of one body are visible between the hips of the other, locked mouths surround a forked-looking tongue, and the female belly sits atop a telescope. These varied, blue-green, hollow forms of the act of love surround the solid human bodies that produce them, which are scarcely discernible except as a dark core around which the sphere shines and coruscates, like tubes of blown glass continually emerging around a hidden mouth.

You're looking at Air Liner microbes. Mammals having sex produce biochemical triggers attracting the Air Liners (otherwise, they might be seen around people and animals who aren't having sex). But if chemistry draws the Air Liners to us, what creates the glowing sculptures in our bedrooms is electricity—specifically, van der Waals forces. These are the most relaxed, mellow forces of electrical attraction. Van der Waals forces get a lot of work done in the world, more by seduction than compulsion—they're very far from the death grip of strong nuclear forces, or the wedlock of chemical bonds. What van der Waals forces feel like, I'd guess, is like knowing that you can resist something and doing it anyway. Here is what they do for Air Liners.

Imagine a human body passing through air, leaving behind it, very briefly, a human-shaped tunnel. A hand would make a five-fingered tunnel as it traveled. But since air is a dense mix of particles and creatures—dust, spores, bacteria—as our skin passes through this thick mixture, it leaves behind a fleeting electrical wake made of charged molecules. We're like spoons going through pudding, leaving a sticky, hollow wake. Air Liners get stuck to this electrical wake of our moving bodies by van der Waals forces. Once they're stuck, the show begins. A few Air Liners sticking to the hollow wake of a human body will explode, in a second, into colonies carpeting the entire tunnel and glowing like wildfire. They are creatures that generate light—bioluminescence—the same light seen during a red tide event, when ocean waves look floodlit from within; the difference is that Air Liners light up the tunnels in air. If the same body passes again through the same spot, backtracking—as people do on the limited area of their beds—the Air Liners will simply carpet the new wake. This accounts for the multiple and overlapping body parts in the glowing spherical sculpture.

Why do Air Liners flock to our bedrooms? The faint charge that we create helps Air Liners depolarize their cell walls, to split themselves into new generations. As we couple in pairs, they divide by the billions. Why do they like mammals? I'd guess the attraction is our fur, or hair, because of what I once noticed after a New Year's Eve party. Lying in a dark room, before a dying fire, I saw a golden line around the shadowy profile of my body. The same nimbus-like line was tracing my lover's recumbent form, in which no features could be seen. We were two black forms outlined in a thin thread of energy, two human-shaped eclipses. Squinting hard, I saw that the sparkly look of the line was due to a near-imperceptible flickering where our body down was agitated by air currents. This was my first sighting of Air Liners after the party, so to say—Air Liners whose bioluminescence was fading from blue-green into lower, red-gold frequencies, as they settled like tired migrating birds onto the sturdy stalks of human body down.

There are so many questions about invisible animals that I cannot answer without the help of science. How many species of Air Liners exist? Do their populations differ from place to place, mammal to mammal, even person to person? Might they accompany each individual—be it human, dog, cat, or mouse—in dedicated colonies, throughout his or her sexual life? Imagine that! Your personal Air Liners, like the chorus of a Greek drama in which you played the starring role, revealing the shapes of your secret acts.

But even if people besides me could see these invisible followers, and were curious enough to take notes during the heat of their embraces, I doubt we'd learn much about what we are from Air Liners. They illumine what we were a moment ago. They show the river we have stepped out of. At the core of their airy, translucent sphere is the solid, dark point of our presence—a point always in the present moment, from which we are thrown toward and into each other, in irresistible collisions. Love is always happening for the first time. And whatever makes it like that is a mystery streaming down from our proper persons into the river of all life, in unbroken shadow.

Imperiled and Extinct
Invisible Beasts

I

A poem called "The Kraken" by Tennyson describes a monster of the ocean bed, over which loom "huge sponges of millennial growth and height." It didn't occur to Tennyson that the Kraken itself might be a sponge, but that is what I deduce from observations and a tiny sample. I discovered the Kraken while on a trip to Antarctica with my sister, who generously invited me to join a research expedition to collect ice core samples. In return for making myself generally useful, I got to observe snorting leopard seals, projectile-pooping penguins, and barnacled whale tails within inches of my nose; and to feel the strange thrill when a ship disappears into the frigid pink dusk, leaving your group to fend for itself. One day, hiking on a glacier, we climbed, one by one, into a deep crevasse—the kind that John Muir was tempted to die in because it resembled the mind of God, assuming that God's thinking is fluorescent blue. In there—suspended like a spider by ropes, pulleys, and ice screws—I hacked off, with my ice ax, a tiny tip of Kraken. Nobody else in our group saw it; I asked them all, later. Nobody had seen anything like that.

The Antarctic Glass Kraken

Antarctica is huge. Not that other places aren't huge, too, but this snowbound continent devoid of human cities seems as huge as the winds, bare of any distraction from its icy vastness. To grasp the southern continent's scale, and picture the climate changes happening there, we often resort to comparisons with the civilized world. When the Larsen-B Ice Shelf collapsed in 2003, glaciologists groping for the right words said that it was like Rhode Island turning to water. How apt for such times, I thought, when Providence seems all too fluid. And where does a state-sized Antarctic ice mass go when it melts? Into an undersea trough, scientists tell us, that is twice the size of Texas. That figures. Twice Texas must be just the size of hell, so I don't wonder that by Antarctic standards, it's getting warm down there.

It's so warm that the Wilkins Ice Shelf, which collapsed during the writing of this book, is the first documented breakup of an Antarctic ice shelf during winter. A short time ago, fifteen thousand square kilometers of

Wilkins was clinging to the mainland by a thin beam of ice, like somebody who has stepped out of a fortieth-floor window and is hanging onto a ledge by one arm. Wilkins's ice arm was a mere three miles wide, but recently it broke up again and is now about one mile wide. So it goes.

When the Antarctic ice melts—when 70 percent of the world's water, and eight hundred thousand years of its ice-locked memories, turn to flood—we will see the Glass Kraken revealed.

The Kraken is a glass sponge: a *Hexactinellida*, the most common sea-bottom-dwelling creature in Antarctica's chilly waters. The ordinary glass sponge is a fairy-tale creature, a glass horn of plenty that spins itself, sometimes extruding branches like diaphanous sleeves. Most are no more than a foot long, but the Kraken is the regal exception. It is very big. Picture a map of Antarctica and you're looking at the Kraken. It grows from a thin layer of water lying between the base of the Antarctic ice cap and the continental bedrock. The Kraken has been growing for a long time, with ice and snow gradually settling in and around and on top of it; its tallest branches are supported by the ice, which froze into place as they followed the water layer. Possibly, the Kraken began as separate communities of glass sponges that merged into a single, gigantic colonial sponge.

If you could look through the imblued walls of glacial chasms (and if you could see invisible beasts), you'd be dumbstruck at the vision of the Kraken's branches sprawling like exurbs and subdivisions off the megalopolis of its body proper. Like all glass sponges, the Kraken conducts electricity, and in the darkness of the bedrock, faint, boreal lights pulse across its webs. In its entirety, it would look like the nighttime panorama from an airplane descending over Manhattan, Tokyo, or some fabled imperial seat—Atlantis City before it drowned.

Yet the Kraken is merely an animal; a sponge, so primitive it hardly qualifies as an animal. Did I say "its body"? Sponges have no body organs, no muscles, no nerves, no digestive systems. Whereas a microscopic water flea has the same striated muscle cells that you have. Such sophistication is light-years beyond your ordinary sponge, which is, basically, an entropy-reducing pocket in the water that perpetuates itself. And this unconscious thing, this jelly without a belly, makes glass—a major industrial product—the way you make daydreams, effortlessly, under the cold deep ocean.

How does the Kraken survive in ice? Sponges normally consume organic particles suspended in water. But the Kraken partners with special bacteria that happily coat the undersides of glaciers. These bacteria coat the Kraken's incurrent canals, and in exchange for safe housing, they supply the Kraken with all the energy it needs. Nothing is impossible if you know the right bacteria—not even a primitive animal the size of a civilization.

When the polar ice caps become polar puddles, Antarctica's stony desert will stand naked. Perhaps, by then, others beside myself will confess to seeing invisible beasts. If they do, we should all hire a boat and go have a look at the Kraken. We won't need rabbit-fur hoods anymore to shield ears from frostbite, and lungs from ice motes. But if the world is still making gas masks, we'll need them against the poisoned miasma of decayed Kraken. I suspect it will be nighttime, the long night of the Pole. I imagine it like this.

There's the dark firmament, and across the stars, the green twisting beams of the southern lights. And the Kraken, exposed. Someone remarks that it looks like acres and acres of construction, all the scaffoldings raised and the beams in place, but smashed by a meteor or an earthquake. Someone else comments, in a morose tone, that while the Kraken looks man-made, it was just an innocent, peaceful animal trying to live in its niche. Our cities, our human civilization, destroyed it. To compare the Kraken to anything man-made is an offense against nature, blurts this morose person. Everybody starts honking out various opinions through the rubber snouts of our gas masks until we feel better or worse. A journalist records our comments. Meanwhile, the boat churns slowly past the view. Silhouetted by the unearthly green aurora, as far as the eye can see, rise the endless, skeletal skylines through which the stars shine.

2

I n selecting material for this book, it was necessary to exclude my ancestors' abundant accounts, though I have made use of them. An exception is the following tale compiled from Granduncle Erasmus's notes. Erasmus was a well-traveled man. Starting out in the merchant marine service at the turn of the twentieth century, he became an itinerant jack-of-all-trades, picking up odd jobs in ports around the world, often trekking inland on the fringes of a scientific expedition—zoological, geological, archaeological. In the notes written on these trips, he always disguised the names of destinations, perhaps to protect the expeditions from rivals or treasure hunters. He would label places with exotic names impossible to find on a map, usually names of women. I chose this tale, not only as a fond tribute to my late predecessor, but also because I was able to see and independently verify the existence of the invisible spider. I have made some additions to fill out and connect his notes, including a comment on the spider I witnessed; the latter is in square brackets and signed "Sophie." I do not know the location of the city called Theodora, which vaguely resembles Washington, DC.

The Spiders of Theodora

THE CITY SWALLOWED by an earthquake was a planned city; the earthquake was not in its plan. Had the city's story ended there, it would have left us with only a trite human irony. Instead, its legacy is a natural wonder: a lost city imprisoned within the invisible domed web of gladiator spiders.

If any city had to be taken over by spiders, Theodora fit the bill. It was originally designed in the shape of a web, with broad, radial avenues crisscrossed by concentric rings of streets. The idea was to make the city airy, light, and easily navigable—like a spider's web; and on many strands of this handsome metropolis glittered, like dewdrops, impressive bronze and alabaster monuments. Equestrian princes, generals with cocked rifles, saints with melded palms stood posturing along every citizen's daily rounds. Armies marched on a thousand carved pediments above tireless caryatids. Every day in that city dawned through a mist of its memories, and the sun, with a tropical glare, reflected off the faces of the famous dead. Although Theodora was not ancient, it loved to commemorate the past, and did so with youthful exuberance.

AT THE CENTER OF THEODORA's urban web was its proudest edifice, the Commonwealth Baths. Modeled on ancient Roman baths, the Commonwealth brought all segments of society together. Any ragpicker who paid admission might leave a tattered T-shirt in the same row of lockers (decorated with cast-iron, dolphin-riding nymphs) where a minister's valet was hanging a swank suit—although the valet, carefully setting out pumice and brushes on a monogrammed folding bench, would keep a sharp eye on the ragpicker. The Commonwealth was democratic in a middling sort of way, below the standard of the Israeli kibbutz but above the US federal tax code. Everyone's feet, whether pedicured and sleek or callused and rough, could steep in the scalding baths and prune in the cold plunges together. As in Rome, the baths offered many enjoyments. You could work out at a gym, go shopping, meet friends, make the rounds of taverns. You could hear a political debate or a concert. You could even hire a mechanic to ride out to the magnificent crescent of parking structures surrounding the Commonwealth and give your car a tune-up while you bathed. But these amenities were accessory to the main ceremonial purpose of the baths, which was the promotion of public memory as much as public hygiene. As soon as you stepped out of your clothes and into the warming room, where you sat on a wooden bench as comforting as a loaf out of the oven—to adjust yourself to higher temperatures—your eyes rested on memorial after memorial of the city's venerable history. Statues of heroes sweated condensation from their straining visages. Philosophers peered into volumes of shining granite from which mists curled. In the cold baths, quaintly lettered texts of the city's founding principles rippled along the mosaic floors of the clear, echoing pools, obscured by foam thrashed up by the clean-limbed citizenry. In the sauna, each red-hot stone was carved to symbolize a problem that the city had once faced, conquered, and sent (as it were) to hell: a foe, a plague, a deflated currency. The crisp, heavyweight public towels were bordered with embroidered dates; you wrapped your body in the calendar of the past. What a proud city it was! How it loved to commemorate the past! What a strange fate befell it!

Now, AS YOU MIGHT HAVE GUESSED, the city planned in the shape of a web was friendly to spiders. Its folklore celebrated them, in fact, perhaps because so many kinds of spiders lived in the city. If, on a summer's night, a young couple neared a park bench perfect for kissing where a three-inch wolf spider crouched, the young man did not try to slay the monster. He would wave one hand like a flag of peace, and the wolf spider (who always hides from people) would slink from her hunting perch with a wary air about her eight-leggy figure. A spider's egg sac in your window was considered good luck; you could buy fake ones. I should add that Theodora was a seat of government, in which the opposition party had always been called the "fishing spiders," because, like their namesakes, they had to run on water to get back into power. Members of the Sex Workers Union, always an important pacesetter in a political town, liked to wear cleavage-catching pendants in the shape of bolas spiders, who toss hormone-soaked lures in the direction of male moths and rope in their sex-befuddled prey. Spies, of which the city had an abundance, both native and foreign, were creepily nicknamed ant spiders, after the arachnid spooks who infiltrate ant colonies by walking on six of their eight legs, waving two forelegs to simulate antennae. And no garden was considered complete without its plump, spiny, orange orb-weaver spider hanging in the middle of a spiral web, treading along the non-sticky threads, dodging the sticky ones, and adding to that mysterious stripe that looks like a gossamer zipper and cannot be explained by human science. That's why people liked it.

IRONICALLY, THEODORA TOOK NO NOTICE of the gladiator spider, a uniquely talented spider that lived there in large numbers. This is not the same as the Namibian *Palfuria gladiator*, so named for the male's extra-large palp. No, these gladiator spiders are invisible, which explains why they went unnoticed despite their extraordinary skills. Like the gladiators of ancient Rome, they fight with nets, throwing a web around their prey and imprisoning it in a domed structure. Unlike other net-casting spiders, who wrap their prey like a sandwich, gladiators create domes so tough and rigid that the vibrations of the struggling prey within cannot be sensed by other spiders in the neighborhood. This is a clever way to discourage food thieves. It follows, therefore, that the gladiator spider herself is also exquisitely sensitive to vibrations. For instance, like the fishing spider, she can sense the vibrations created on the surface of the water by small swimming prey. Sometimes she detects and dives for tadpoles or newly hatched minnows, spinning an underwater dome that captures a small air bubble along with the catch, giving the spider an air tank. Gladiator spiders are barely an inch across, but very brave: they eagerly tackle big game. A gladiator spider can, in fact, capture a stag beetle the size of your middle finger.

[I saw this happen on television during a political debate between two candidates for high office. The mortal combat took place on top of one of the candidate's toupees—that's how I could tell that it was a toupee, because anyone with real hair would have felt something. You really can't have a big angry beetle, waving its claws, imprisoned on the top of your head under a silk yarmulke woven on the spot by a very active spider and continue gabbing on about faith and family and values as if nothing unusual were happening, unless you are wearing a toupee—a stiff one.—Sophie.]

ON A CLEAR SEPTEMBER DAY, an earthquake swallowed the city whole, from the tips of the obelisks to the bolts on the manholes, in less time than it takes to read this sentence, and the city's founders, had they still been alive, might have written with a flourish, FINIS; but Mother Nature's work is never finished.

In those horrifying first seconds, Theodora came apart in large segments like a dropped layer cake; districts that had been adjacent were now perpendicular. A smothered death-scream tore through the earth, from the mouths of everyone trying to find out where he or she was. The composer never lived who could imagine what it sounded like—and never should. Every creature on two or four feet fell down and slowly asphyxiated. Pigeons, sparrows, hawks, robins, cardinals, orioles, and flycatchers dropped out of the black air like suicides; dogs, cats, raccoons, mice, squirrels, chipmunks, snakes, toads, a few mangy coyotes, and a lone black bear tumbled or crept to their deaths. Even the rats died. Bacteria began their long feast. In the Commonwealth Baths, whose skylights were plugged with total darkness, the spacious, venerable pools and graceful porticos seethed and dripped scum as the clear waters of health became tarry sumps of skeletons.

Yet, for a time, curiously, Theodora was full of life. Had a human being been able to witness the aftermath of the catastrophe, he or she might have reflected that as Rome was saved by its cackling geese, so this buried city was preserved by its gladiator spiders, in one of the greatest feats any creature has ever performed.

WHEN THE EARTHQUAKE HIT and the city roared down into the earth's canyon jaws, the gladiator spiders resorted to their three great gifts: sensitivity, engineering, and courage. Clinging to the city, they sensed its seismic shudders, and they gauged the giant size of this new vibration, while their body hair picked up the scent of edible tissue trapped inside the city's crumpled architecture. To the spiders, the event felt exactly as if the world's biggest prey animal had challenged them to a match. Bravely, they rose to the challenge. In an unprecedented move, every gladiator spider joined with its fellows and began to spin a web of scale. Perhaps they'd been social creatures all along but hadn't needed to band together before—or perhaps it was a fluke, a one-in-a-billion chance that they would all start spinning simultaneously. Either way, the gladiator spiders' consortium, in the very teeth of catastrophe, spun with as much cool purpose as if every pumping, leaping, twirling little spinner had been possessed by the ghost of Buckminster Fuller. Soon the whole shaking city was encased in a vaulted silk dome with air pinned inside it. There wasn't enough oxygen to save the people or animals (except for the kinds of worms that breathe the air in dirt). There was enough air, however, to save temporarily the gladiator spiders, thanks to their book lungs. Book lungs are how spiders breathe: layered blocks of tissue, like tiny books, through the "pages" of which gases percolate. In gladiator spiders, the pages are very thin and densely packed, like little Norton anthologies of literature, allowing oxygen to be used more efficiently than in other spiders' book lungs, which resemble quickly read best sellers. That is the reason why, after the buried city's other beasts had perished, the gladiator spiders, armed with an encyclopedic breathing apparatus and the courage of intellectuals fighting the death of their ideals, stayed alive. While they lived, they kept spinning. They went after the edible tissue inside the ruins—the corrupt flesh of animals and people—and roped, levered, tugged, and suspended in their silken larders whatever they found to subsist on. Multitudes of skeletons were thus hoisted upward, into the great dome, like bones in the vision of the prophet Ezekiel, who saw a valley of skeletons rise and stand again. But these bones did more than stand. They levitated. Like angels and swans swung through opera theaters on invisible ropes, they hung in the dense mesh of the gladiator spiders' webs.

Now, recollect that if you were to see the city inside the earth, you would not see the gladiator spiders or their webs. You would see only the image of a meta-memorial: a memorial to memorials. You would see Theodora's monuments—those alabaster and bronze statues that used to glitter along its avenues—collapsed in violent heaps where the saint's nose is rammed against the cracked breast of Justice, and commanding hands, as heavy as motors, point from under buckled pavements and open expressively out of crushed walls. If you will pardon the comparison, imagine a snow globe with the monuments as its plastic scene and the disconnected bones as snow. It's like that, except that the city doesn't shake anymore, while the bones, secured by natural causes, float forever in place.

3

Animals can teach us, and the Foster Fowl was the most extraordinary teacher alive. It hurts to think that I may have had a hand in its disappearance, and when my conscience starts to prick, I go over the whole episode inch by inch . . . all the way up the "escalator to extinction."

The Foster Fowl

GO OUT ON A JULY DAY, when from a high branch a robin pours out its carol like a general blessing, along with a flycatcher's whoop, an oriole's note, and the melody of a song sparrow that springs alike from earth and air. Go out, take a pair of kitchen shears. You can smell the tall milkweeds, with their flowering globes like old-fashioned microphone heads; they're broadcasting a summer special that brings in the bees, bent double with effort, and the monarch butterflies who have mated tipsily in the air and now, female by female, stately orange and black-deckled, land to lay their eggs. Across your path, a hummingbird arches in an inch-long arabesque—with a diminutive roar she chases off a wren, trailing her battle cry:

Squeaksneeterie!

Go to the purple lavender smoking on its naked stems. Respecting the bees, whose business here is more important than yours, cut yourself a bundle, take it home, wash it, cram it into a clean Ball jar, and fill the jar with honey. Seal it tight and take it across the road to your neighbor's farmhouse. Exchange it for a half-dozen eggs lifted out from under their mamas, still warm, and take them home on a chipped plate that you set on your porch corner, just inside the screen door. And she'll come. Or she would till lately.

You won't see her actually arrive. If the eggs are placed out for her, she'll just be there, like the Beatles song about Mother Mary: "When I offer chocolates, she is standing right in front of me." Although I misheard that song: "In my hour of darkness" were the correct words, but I always thought that Mother Mary would come when you made her an offering suitable to her place in the natural scheme of things. If you put out a golden box of fine chocolates, like the platform of a Byzantine throne, she would appear, drawn to the odor of your prayer, her blue mantle brushing the lid, her eyes piercingly gentle.

Anyway . . . put the eggs out, and soon, in that humble porch corner, a creature appears like an azure wave from some transparent sea, mantling the eggs and crooning, *cro-coo-roc, cro-coo-roc.* As you recover from her stunning plumage—peacock, aqua, lacustrine—you see that she's rather comical. Her build is between a pheasant and a small wild turkey. Her neck is a lapis pipe; she fixes on you a gaze the color of pineapple meat; her short, curved, turquoise beak resembles nothing so much as a pair of plastic-coated sewing scissors. She has no hard feathers, but is entirely covered in iridescent down—a silken mop, a turkey shawled in sapphire threads, and over her head droops a crest like an unraveled pompon. And she's as soft inside as out: she can't resist a clutch of foundling eggs. But unlike any other mother bird, she won't defend her nest.

So begin the game: steal her eggs, her newly adopted chicken children, by scattering corn outside. She'll unseat herself like a shimmering cloud, rise on indigo stilts, bend her long feet as if inserting them into high-heeled pumps, and quickly tiptoe out the door to graze, for she's very hungry. When your Foster Fowl returns to find her eggs in your hands, she doesn't rush you screaming or stab her blue beak in your blood. Instead she glides to the trees bordering your yard, teeters there, a silvery teardrop, and melts away into the forest. Now, now she is your quarry to be pursued with eager questions. How many species, and which, will the Foster Fowl incubate? How many avian species owe a boost, and how many abandoned broods owe their success, to a mother whose all-enfolding love does not discriminate between her kind and others?

I LIVE NEAR A SPOT known as the Warbler Capital of the World. In spring, bird fanciers from all over converge here, on a boardwalk surrounded by marshes, to jostle fiercely for position, sometimes even erecting their camera tripods over the heads of other birders who have knelt down to peer into the brush, binoculars at the ready, oblivious. Complete strangers, standing cheek by jowl, exchange intelligence on the likeliest location of the blue-headed vireo or the ruby-crowned kinglet. Men dressed like hunters tote weapon-sized lenses; old couples bicker in soft voices over their lists of "life birds"—a life bird is one that you see for the very first time. Ten years ago, it didn't occur to me that the first Foster Fowl to visit my porch—my own life bird, whom I nicknamed "My Blue Heaven"— was anything but an accidental. Something soars overhead looking for Nova Scotia: that's an accidental. But My Blue Heaven wasn't, after all, an accidental: she hadn't gone out of her way at all. She was a harbinger.

I'd discovered My Blue Heaven brooding a plateful of new eggs I'd laid down momentarily, and the game came about by accident. When she fled into the woods, I decided to track her. Since she was obviously flightless, the best method was to seek the nests of birds that laid their eggs on the ground, and might attract her. While consulting Peterson's long list of these, I noticed something curious: many birds were shifting their ranges northward. I should have thought! Birds as different as the tiny blue-gray gnatcatcher and the lumbering turkey vulture were moving northward. Why didn't I put two and two together? What was I thinking?

I ought, I ought to have wondered what a blatantly southern bird like My Blue Heaven, with her morpho butterfly looks and her uselessness for winter, was doing near Lake Erie. She must have walked, maybe all the way from Florida. And after her, I saw only females (except, memorably, once). Why? Why didn't I mull it over? Because I was stupid. Because I was having too much fun, finding out which eggs the Foster Fowls mothered, as if nature had developed a new summer sport for my benefit. *All for me,* I gloated, setting the lure of the orphan eggs, sprinkling the trail of corn, and finding the world's most beautiful blues in a downy cloud. *All for me,* the thrill of tracking. How many of us are philosophical enough to question the whys and wherefores of a pleasure? I wasn't, as I hot-footed it into the summer woods. *All for me.* Imbecile.

To FIND A FOSTER FOWL in the greenwood wasn't easy, because only in pursuit of a blue creature does one appreciate how much blue there is in green. Where eyes failed I tried ears, parting the brush between trees, listening. *Phew!* called the veeries back and forth, and *Freebie! freebie!* screamed the phoebe, and *Truly to thee,* sang the bluebirds, and the killdeer, whose species is *Vociferus,* was, and *Wheat, wheat, wheat to you,* sang a cardinal whose babies shrilled *Feed-me-feed-me-feed-me-feed-me.* I went to the marsh around my pond, and spent hours crouched under tickling grasses, binoculars glued to my eye sockets. The pond, at the bottom of a quarry, continuously reflected a quivering, linear, blue light that caressed the stone walls, and where the walls met the water stood cattails and reeds. That's where I found My Blue Heaven. For weeks, I studied the volitional shimmer that gave her away, that wasn't sky or water or light, but a maternal breast. I grew very curious, because no pheasant can swim like a duck . . . but when the time came, there it was: a bobbing chain of ducklings, dabbling, shaking their baby rumps, in the ripples and on the sand beside My Blue Heaven's hiding place.

In later years, I followed my egg-deprived Foster Fowls to the nests of mute swans, Canada geese, woodcocks, whippoorwills, bobwhites, and once, a kingfisher, and never discovered how they did it—how they taught the young of other species. But somehow, they did.

In those years, I could count on three or four Foster Fowls in a summer. I never saw their chicks: not one blue puffball, and I wondered (though not enough*). Where were their mates? A pheasant female wandering, all alone, in search of abandoned eggs—why didn't this bother me more? Such birds live in harems with a territorial male. Nature doesn't make roving bachelor hens. Of course, invisible animals can be very different from their visible counterparts, but it was still odd. I knew that My Blue Heaven was an invisible bird because I'd tried to photograph her, but the pictures showed only an assortment of ducks, swans, geese, woodcocks, and other ordinary birds.

---

* I did try to find out if Foster Fowl chicks were being hatched out here by tweezing apart the regurgitated pellets lying under owl nests. I probed the pellets of short-eared owls, great horned owls, and Owls of Aurora (invisible owls that hunt at daybreak, although their skills are far more suited to nocturnal hunting, so they don't do too well, but never learn any better). No owls were regurgitating Foster Fowl bones.

For some reason, invisible animals do not show up on camera. It is a great handicap to amateur naturalists of invisible wildlife, like myself, and it is a great pity. Especially considering what ultimately happened.

One day, I found my royal cloud sitting in a dent in the grass, barely a nest, on a clutch of creamy eggs that I glimpsed when she rose to turn them with her deft turquoise beak. I stared till my eyes watered, in the shadows where a pebbled sort of whistle announced a single, obsessed cricket.

"You crazy girl," I thought, "you insane bird. This, I have got to see."

And I did see, soon afterward—on my computer screen, as I scanned the photographs taken by my infrared camera. These pictures explained why the Foster Fowl needs to be invisible. Otherwise, she'd be a meal for the young owl caught—wings perpendicular between tree trunks—clutching a limp cardinal. How had she reared this raptor, whose habits were the cruel opposite of her own? How mysterious was the being that I hunted through summer after summer, her loving kindness as abundant as the air. My instincts became honed to clues I was not conscious of—hunches of the feet, guesses of the inner compass—that led me into ever deeper concealments, obscurer hiding places. I gagged at the sapphire on a ripe, torn corpse, crooning her cradle song as if a vulture's nest were purest myrrh . . .

Ten years ago, I saw my last Foster Fowl. It was an August morning. The bells, rattles, and whistles in the insect world rose into a sky stuffed with pale flames. *Thwock!* A walnut smacked the turf, just missing my skull. Hello, gravity and time. I felt suddenly fed up with gravity and time and their boring threats; I felt put upon by natural law, and went into the woods swinging a long stick to sweep away the spiderwebs that I really had no business to ravage, given how excellent an animal a spider is. With that arrogance of ours, like some pompous bureaucrat in a Byzantine procession, I marched through the woods swaying my stick in front of me, tearing down what I couldn't see and didn't want to. I marched into a stand of oaks about four inches high. Each green shoot spread a top cluster of five large leaves, like a puppy's big paws. A stand of mighty oaks was trying to grow up here. Then I saw my Foster Fowl, in the spattered light. Her neck was sunk in her breast, while her candy-yellow eyes, swiveling toward me, registered broodiness, the mother love that belongs so completely to birds. (Only domestic hens are unmotherly, because we've bred it out of them.) Her throat inflated as she crooned. She looked as if a valve had opened beneath her nest, inside the earth where it was still a molten star, and was shooting a warm ray through her heart. After a while, she cranked up on her indigo stilts, shook out her wings, and went pecking among the infant oaks. I fiddled with the focus adjustment and heard my own voice, spontaneous as any birdcall:

Oh no! Oh shit! Oh, no.

And it was stupid to have marched over, crunching leaf litter under my boots. Stupid to have knelt by the woven nest-cup, putting my big human paw there, tossing eggs into the woods, good riddance to bad eggs, to thuggish cowbirds. I detest cowbirds. For every cowbird egg stealing space in another species' nest, there's one more disappointment in the world. Okay, and it was stupid to have panicked when I found myself electrified, on my feet, backing away from a three-foot-high chunk of enraged lapis lazuli with ruby eyes and crimson crest, stretching out his wicked long neck with a blue beak and a black tongue hollering like a turkey on the warpath, *Rotter-rotter-rotter-rotter-rotter-rotter-rotterrrrr!* I took to my heels. Laugh if you like, it was terrible. I had finally met a male Foster Fowl. There was nothing soft in his feathers or his comportment. I'll never know whether it was he and his mate who wove the nest with that last, sole egg . . . that last egg at the bottom of the nest, which may, or may not, have been a Foster Fowl's. I came back later. The nest was moved. I don't blame them. I will never know.

THE NEXT SUMMER, I set out my chicken-egg lure: no Foster Fowl came, though raccoons did. I waited all summer. The summer after that, I set out eggs again: no Foster

Fowl came, though raccoons did and trashed my porch with my own trash. I spent the summer lurking in all her usual spots; I watched the poor, bare eggs, in many an abandoned nest, snatched up by squirrels, crunched down by foxes, engulfed by snakes. And the summer after that. And the summer after that.

When my summer fun appeared to be gone, I did what all humans do when their fun is gone. I looked around for something to blame. I picked up the phone and called Evie, who as a biologist was interested in the whole story, up to my sighting of the male Foster Fowl, and as a sibling, was amused at the thought of her older sister acting like a nitwit.

"Wow, that was really stupid," she said. "Cowbirds are evil? Compared to, like, *humans*?"

"Do you think they'll ever come back?" I begged.

"Um, Sophie, I would guess that your birds are over-producing females, which species do in hard times. And this heavily female population is moving north, because their habitat's screwed up. That's what ornithologists call the *escalator to extinction*."

I imagined an escalator on which grinning human skeletons, clutching handbags, rose into a dark department store.

"What that means," Evie continued, "is like, birds follow the plants and animals they eat into cooler climates.

The farther north they go, the worse they do, because they're going into conditions for which they haven't evolved. The thing is, your females don't sound very weather-resistant. So if they're dying in the winters up here, that puts, like, more pressure on the species. Which, in response, produces even more females, who die in the winter. You follow?"

"Yes," I said, repressing the urge to say I wasn't stupid, because I was.

"The species gets thinned out. It's a vicious circle. If climate change weren't happening so fast, maybe they'd adapt. Like, a mutation could produce hard-feathered females who could survive the cold. As it is . . ." A near-audible shrug. "Some of my colleagues think that global warming will wipe out like thirty percent of land-bird species in this century."

"Are you joking?" I croaked. "Look, I know you think I'm crazy. But please."

"You," laughed my sister, "totally have an imagination. And you care about animals. You know what I think? Without imagination, we can't stop extinction. That's the main problem with getting people mobilized. Thirty percent of land birds—it's not just about, oh, I don't see my woodpeckers at the feeder, oh, I can't bag my pheasant, whatever. It's not about fun. It's about survival. Because a bird touches so much—the plants it pollinates, the organisms it eats, the predators, the whole incredible cascade of species it affects. I mean, mass extinction is incredibly dangerous. But for most people—hey, the world is full of animals, the sky is full of birds, like—nobody has to imagine life without them." Evie spoke with passion, which made her sound like someone with pressing errands to run. I was standing in the sunlit porch, phone in hand, hanging my head. Shadows of leaves trembled over the stone floor, as if fossil leaves, embedded in the slate, were struggling to surface.

THE BLAME FOR LOSING the Foster Fowl fell squarely on me, the only human being who had seen her, yet taken her for granted. Why hadn't I trapped one, built a rookery, nurtured a breeding pair? Why hadn't I used my special gift of seeing the invisible to protect what others couldn't see? It would have been no more than what naturalists and biologists do when they try to protect some unsung creature performing the work of life, some necessary being that lacks the allure of a politician's face, an entertainer's breasts, or a soldier's corpse. The longer I reflected, the larger loomed the loss. I missed my fun, then I mourned the Foster Fowl's absence in the world and would have been overjoyed to know, sight unseen, that she still existed, rearing the abandoned young of others. Then, gradually, the grandeur of the chance that I had squandered became apparent. If My Blue Heaven could teach a duck to swim, an owl to hunt, and a vulture to scavenge, what might a human being have learned from her? We don't really know what we're fit for, what human nature really is or might be, but we do know that our nature fits into the space created by all the other animals, a particular wisdom learned among them, and the Foster Fowl was the best teacher of them all. Too late!

Reader, when I die, and my soul goes to be weighed, when my soul is weighed as the Egyptians prophesied, on a scale against the weight of truth itself—a single feather—which way will those scales tip? I don't know. You tell me.

4

Picture this allegory: *Two angels stand on either side of Evolution's throne, each holding a symbol. Competition holds a lamp that, like a predator's eyes, shines on the circle of creatures favored by natural selection. Symbiosis holds the rainbow, whose arch spans the horizon of the living earth. Around Symbiosis's feet grow flowering plants that co-evolved with pollinating animals. Symbiosis's trailing sleeve is beaded with tiny eukaryotic cells, from whose merging of bacteria and archaea all the earth's plants and animals spring. Without Competition—chaos. Without Symbiosis—nullity. This is a tale on the side of Symbiosis, and I have mentioned angels because when I ponder the existence of the soul and spiritual things, I think of Beanie Sharks.*

Beanie Sharks

IT WAS ON THE TOP FLOOR of a natural history museum, where they keep the artifacts of oceanic tribes, on a rainy afternoon. There were pools of light, and in one of them a display case, and near it a bench on which I sank in disbelief. I went back up to the case, put my hands in my pockets, craned forward again, reread the typed labels. I stared at the remains of an animal that had been mis-classified as "ritual object, or toy." Then I returned to the bench and tried to absorb what I had seen, hanging my wrists over my knees and staring at the floor. To know that an extinction is coming and be unable to sound an alarm, because the creature is invisible ... But most beasts are invisible, more or less—people don't know about them, or don't pay attention to them, and then they disappear, invisible forever and to everyone. It's no consolation to think that even if most people saw invis-ible beasts, they still might not care.

I got up again, went over to the display case, and looked at the remains again, the way you look and look at the accessories of a pet who has died. Or the way people look at a stuffed extinct animal, like a moa, arranged by a taxidermist to seem capable of coming back to life, so that we lower our voices and suppress notes of wonder, as if the beast could hear us, which is what we really want—after all, our murmurs tell the stuffed corpse, we can see you, know you, so you must be here, not altogether gone? Surely you are still somehow here? But the stuffed thing doesn't move from its wired spot in the museum diorama. Thanks to the longevity of museums it will likely outlast us, and when we're dead and buried and in the carbon cycle, it will be still sitting with its moth-eaten fur, its desiccated feathers, its upholstery scales. Of all humanity's monuments—ideas, structures, artworks, devices—the ones that represent us most enduringly are those unique and eternal absences, the extinctions.

I knew this animal. It looked like a beige porcelain Frisbee, and was the shell of a giant limpet attached, in life, to a much bigger, invisible beast. Half a partnership lay in the display case, between visible and invisible. Morosely fingering the plastic museum pass that couldn't be shredded, and shouldn't be chewed, I sighed. What if our own bodies had invisible parts, unseen symbiotic partners who helped us function? Not souls, exactly. They would be animals, as real as the invisible Beanie Shark, whose visible partner, the Cap limpet, lay here. The parquetry squeaked as I leaned forward, breathing on the glass. "Unknown ritual object, or toy." I didn't know what made me sadder, the

Cap limpet, sedulously mislabeled—or its Beanie Shark, somewhere in the ocean, bereft of a partnership that after hundreds of millions of years was now dissolving . . .

THE OCEANGOING FISH are hard to know. The original vertebrate lineage, they dwell in life's essential sphere; if you broke the continents and melted the volcanoes down to stubs, nothing much would change for them. Yet when we think of human babies, we ought to think of sharks. They are the animals who most closely resemble us in embryo, reports a Harvard biologist. Shark heads and human heads develop very similarly, from four embryonic scallops called the gill arches. Each gill arch develops into an area of the human, or shark, head; and each gill arch contains genes that direct its development, so that sharks become sharklike, while humans become humanlike. Bones that become jaws in a shark, become ear bones in a human. (A very bad sonnet by Keats says that his ear is open "like a greedy shark"—technically, he wasn't far off.) In embryo, humans, basking sharks, and Beanie Sharks look exactly the same. A Beanie is an invisible basking shark, and would be identical to the visible kind if not for the giant limpet, programmed to grow along with it, that tweaks its genes in embryo. As a result, the Beanie's head is altered slightly. But first let me tell you about basking sharks, those noble fish among whom I've swum while scuba diving off the coast of Scotland.

We do not know how many are left alive. They've been overfished for centuries, thanks to their slowness, lack of aggression, and plethora of uses. We make basking sharks into leather, oil, shark's fin soup, and shark cartilage, a reputed aphrodisiac—ironically, since basking sharks swim in sex-segregated groups, like holy orders, and have been observed to inspect our boats from a distance, not sure, perhaps, if they've detected a potential mate, with all the awkwardness of habitual chastity. There are many things about them that we do not know. Here is a partial list:

1. Why only the right ovary of the female appears fertile,
2. At what age and season, exactly, mating occurs,
3. How often they breed,
4. Whether the gestation period is one, two, or three years,
5. How many young are born to one mother,
6. When they become mature.

What we do know is that basking sharks are creatures of peace. Twenty to forty feet long, they swim slowly, at two knots, their pectoral fins—the analogue of our arms—relaxed, their bodies insinuating a continuous S, with an occasional strong flick of a lunate tail. Their mouths gape to scoop up plankton blooms. Those yawning mouths are cavernous; torrents of water and small life stream through them, like crowds through the pillared portals of medieval cathedrals, which, with the ribbing that soars up their inner cheeks to the vault of their upper jaws, they resemble. Viewed from below, their long-snouted, bulging heads look like shadowy onion domes; from above, their smooth heads are bordered with five gills, like flying buttresses, lined with baleen filters. In immense tranquility they swim, gripped by mighty, unending yawns, perhaps sleeping in motion, for they are very simple: they cannot pump water across their gills and must swim to keep breathing; they lack swim bladders too. They make do with little. They swim into a human imagination like the swelling unison and subsidence of monastic chants, and the devotions of silence.

These inoffensive creatures were officially declared a nuisance, and fished aggressively, by the United States and Canada from 1945 till 1970, but are now protected by several nations.

The Beanie Shark is not protected, though. It suffers from ocean acidification, the result of excess carbon dioxide, as everyone knows. I try not to blame my elected representatives for ignoring my e-mails about this, from my technical-with-bibliographies-attached ones, to my pithy-screaming-caps ones, to my most recent ones headed $&SX4U. I understand that my government is composed of real people, ordinary, real Americans, just like me—as they always insist on TV—so how can they, in their *echt* similarity to me, be expected to solve the very problems I cannot? Anyway!

The oceans are turning acidic, and because of it, creatures who make shells out of calcium carbonate are failing to make shells. Corals that once towered from the ocean floor like titanic conglomerations of rainbows are now dead and bleached. If the imperial corals succumb, what becomes of the humble Cap limpet?

The Cap, about the size of a steering wheel, sits atop the Beanie Shark's enormous head. When the shark rolls over or dives, the Cap stays on, and the monumental fish resembles a member of an old-fashioned lodge with funny headgear. The Cap is anchored by filaments of its digestive tract, which follow grooves in the shark's head leading to its mouth, where they skim off some of the captured plankton. It's an easy berth for the Cap, siphoning its meals from the Beanie Shark's mouth. Yet this limpet is no mere parasite. It helps its giant companion by performing two special tricks.

When plankton blooms run thin, the Cap performs the propeller trick. Attached in an upside-down position, it opens its lid and sticks its foot up in the water. The foot unfolds into four paddlelike limbs, called *parapodia,* that beat the water, creating a whirlpool to trap plankton and lead them toward the shark. Many gastropods that live in the sea have such parapodia: the sea butterfly's foot divides into two pretty, flapping lobes; the sea angel's parapodia look like rosy wings. While the Cap's propeller trick is within the norms of gastropod creativity, its second trick, the bubble wand, is more remarkable. For this trick, the Cap also opens its lid and sticks up its foot, but instead of paddles, it ejects a long string of spherical sacs, made of thin mucus membranes, which puff up into clusters of bubbles. These assist the Beanie Shark in maintaining buoyancy as it swims, though I am not sure what trigger causes the limpet to blow bubbles. Mollusks have their little ways, as any pearl farmer will tell you. One way or another, the Beanie, a simple basking shark with no refinements of its own, knows that when pickings are slim, its symbiont will lend a helping foot.

The Cap has not gone unnoticed by humanity. It washes up on land, from time to time, so I am not surprised that Haeckel drew it—though he called it a "barnacle," and drew dots and paisleys all over it, giving it the dandified appearance of a propeller beanie worn by Oscar Wilde.

IF WE EVER HAD A CHANCE to understand this intriguing pair, the visible limpet and the invisible shark, it is passing with the acidification of the oceans: the Caps are dying, unable to form their calcite shells. For tens of millions of years, this symbiont has tweaked the Beanie's genes, in embryo, ensuring that the shark will develop the limpet's comfortable seat on its head. The exact nature of that process will likely remain a mystery. At a wild guess, it may be connected to the malfunction of the female basking shark's left ovary. Possibly, the Cap influences the growth of all basking sharks, but is only successful with the invisible kind. How can we know, how can we ever understand, when these deft symbionts are cruelly dissolved by the very water that used to nurture their whirling paddles, and their enigmatic, joyous bubbles?

As for the Beanies, well, sharks have been around for a long time and nothing much fazes them. I suppose the Beanies could evolve into a race of invisible basking sharks with slightly deformed heads, and slightly fewer advantages. Yet it's hard to believe that they will not in some fishy sense pine for their loss, when the plankton blooms run thin, or when they're tired and heavy on their fins. Habits favored and selected for, for millions of years, can hardly be shed in a few seasons.

I'm tempted to describe the post-limpet Beanies as lost souls, since they're invisible and have such a spiritual lifestyle. And because they're detached from the visible bodies of their Caps. But that comparison would miss the point. After years of studying invisible animals, I believe that there is no spiritual aspect of our life that is not, simultaneously, animal. And animality is symbiosis. Our bodies are "integrated colonies" of cells, says a renowned biologist; and beyond the mergers of lone cells into animal bodies are the partnerships between animals—the goby cohabiting with a blind shrimp that it assists, the wrasses cleaning parasites from a grouper's jaws. There are the mutual aid societies of all animals with their gut flora. And beyond animality lies the plant kingdom on which animals depend for food, the kingdom of photo-synthesis, which itself sprang from an ancient partnering of blue-green cyanobacteria and eukaryotic cells ... The blooming gardens of earth and sea depend on symbiosis, the sharing-out of life's problems among many kinds of beings and their abilities.[*]

So if our bodies have invisible parts—call them souls—they would surely be animals. They would be the symbionts of a creature who sometimes claims to be the image of God, and in embryo resembles nothing so much as a shark.

---

* "Human beings are integrated colonies of ameboid beings." In *What Is Life?* by Lynn Margulis and Dorion Sagan (Berkeley: University of California Press, 1995) p. 141.

5

The present, or Holocene, mass extinction is not the only one in life's history. It is the only one caused by a single organism capable of seeing the big picture, understanding its own destructive role, and changing that. But we don't see the big picture unless it's shown to us. Once, I had a moment of fortunate epiphany—a moment granted sometimes to naturalists—when the big picture comes overwhelmingly together, and you actually see the meaning of Lynn Margulis's apothegm: "Life is its own inimitable history." If I saw the big picture, though, it wasn't accidental: it was because I had to make a choice.

The Golden Egg

THE DAY COMES WHEN I walk home through a waist-high meadow of panic grass, goldenrod, and lace saucers of wild carrot, and I see, as if I had startled it into being, a plane of green glittering moving leftward like a perturbed school of fish in the clearest of waters. I walk where those newly falling leaves drift by, and have to make up my mind whether a russet flutter in the grass is a monarch butterfly or a dead leaf—the last of its season, or the first? I've been visiting with my neighbor, a farmer, who has found a nest of dead, half-formed bluebirds inside shells so thin they burst at a touch. She's wondering what caused it—no pesticide she's aware of, but who knows, these days, what gets in the water? We both have wells. I've promised to check my birdhouses ... but instead, lazily, I'm climbing down the side of the quarry, gray and cracked as shelves of unfired clay, lichen-rusted, blackened where my sunken pond has burned it with life. Sand curves between the rockface and a peeling carpet of water lilies. A little mite is headed up and down the edges of a lily's petals, so burning white they're gray where a candle flame is blue. Hoof-prints in the mud show where a doe and her spotted fawn have stood, immersed to their hocks, chewing salad; dried lily stems litter the beach. In the water, my head is a brown shadow through which glide the grim torpedo shapes of the pond's top predators, the bass. Poison? When I look up, a crevice in the rock winks, an amber wink, and there is the Golden Egg, never seen before, yet recognizable as nothing else. Many animals live and have lived at my home address, but this one has no peer. In a waxy, ochre body the size of a lychee nut, it holds what the human race craves: riches and longevity.

The—my—Golden Egg is tightly wedged into its crack; I see where the rockwall flaked, a pale scab, to reveal its tawny inhabitant, which has likely sat there since the glacier melted. Should I pluck it out? Should I go get a screwdriver and pry it out? My hand reaches, unsure of its next move; knowing as much as anyone does about Golden Eggs, I'd guess this one needs help. But against the limestone sunned to pumice-gray, my raised hand reminds me of those red handprints in the most primi-tive cave paintings. I don't know much, do I? All around, crickets, katydids, and nameless summer bugs are raising a song like the spinning of bicycle chains, louder and louder. It feels as though the deep past is revolving over the face of the pond, a dazzling wheel, on which tiny images of crea-tures appear and disappear, bringing together a minute Golden Egg and a miniscule human hand for a fraction of a sliver of a second. My spine hairs rise in the breeze; in a moment, the wheel will have turned. I will have done good or ill. In the meantime, it's a story wheel.

The story begins at my home address.

A SHINING, FOUR-FOOT-DEEP ocean, mighty and pretty as Venus, lies across the continent. Corals flower in the place of cities, and all creatures live and die in sunbeams dusted with tiny crustaceans. The Golden Egg is flat, drifting along like scum on a pot of boiled beans. It isn't much; with ambition, it might have been a sponge. But when a trilobite nibbles its edges, our drifter becomes a revolutionary—it rolls into a ball and spins away, sending ripples of frustration through the trim, fringed chitin of its foe. Now that they're aware of each other, nothing is the same, and all the rest follows, all those irreversible changes that go forward on hunger and a touch (whatever it means, to whomever it is happening) within the balance of life; the changes that will make the Golden Egg the most fortunate of animals. Starting with a major extinction. The first land plant, inching up on its rootlet, dropping its seed, forms forests thirty meters deep whose roots, cracking rock, swell streams with minerals, the first fertilizers—until algae smothers the seas, and the surf falling on all shores is a pounding dirge for three quarters of marine species. That is the price of seeds. The trilobites are diminished; in their absence the Golden Egg dares to assume its present size, bobbling along more heartily, eating more, being eaten less ... never to lie flat again, it becomes, like everything, the shape of a relationship. One that's just getting started.

Meanwhile, our ancestors are beginning to make the meeting of a human hand and a Golden Egg possible, as six-foot dragonflies skim the scaled trees snaking up, from roots bedizened with mussels, into the torrential fronds of future coal reserves. Through the shrubbery troop our forebears, four-footed beasts who squat and dig like mad. If your ear was laid to that fat soil, you'd hear the champagne-cork popping of plopping eggs, the rubbery shot with which animals are conquering the land. The price of eggs will be paid in about 290 million years, with another major extinction—look around you! ... But I digress.

In the saw-blade shade of dripping cycads, the Golden Egg makes progress too. It is still life's simpleton, a mere sphere. Only now its soft skin contains a stony bubble, made by the bacteria that mineralize its wastes. Wrapped around its digested and crystallized experience, it has a tougher style, but must face, very soon, the contradictions lurking in self-containment. Meanwhile the earth, too, becomes hard-hearted. From her equator to her poles sprawls the super-continent, Pangea, with its overheated interior, dynastic droughts, burled deserts, and gravel gorges where half-ton creatures trudge along and wave their creaking dorsal sails. Our friend the Golden Egg sometimes gets carted around in a gizzard, waiting to be cracked—an extreme approach to the problem it has now, of being as hard, inside, as firebrick. When it feels sexy, it fertilizes its inner cavity (don't ask) and a second Golden Egg begins forming. But until the parent membrane can be shed, its shell cracked, and its young freed, the two concentric beings suffer in limbo, unable to bring new out of old, rebirth out of fulfillment. A breakthrough is needed, so be grateful for genius in the world!

They have class—trilobites do. They *are* a class. An evolutionary elite, from the get-go they never resembled any other creature except their supremely successful selves, beginning as shiny ovals that curl up with a perfectly interlocking fringe. On this they riff. Barbed, smooth, blind, bugeyed, with legs like running mascara, with heads like scimitars, without heads. They go planktonic and float and have Zen; they go big as your arm and whack the hell out of their prey; and through it all, they lust after, cannot stay away from, cannot stop chasing the Golden Egg. Why does the genus *Walliserops* evolve a vicious trident atop its head? "For male display," suggests a source, but I'm not so sure. Those tridents are Egg forks, the cutlery of the cultist, the maven, the devotee for whom a delicacy holds the very flavor of life. Against the Golden Egg's slippery toughness, the trilobites surpass themselves: gnawing off the outer skin, they let the hard shell turn brittle and crack, and its inner progeny escape. Without their bravura gusto, the Egg has no future; without its toothsome sphere, the trilobites lack temptation. They're made for each other!

But as these things happen, everything changes for the worst.

It cascades like the evil plot that it isn't. Volcanoes spewing lava across Siberia are not foreknown as their basalt cools into black cobbles, the Via Appia of death. Dust clouds are not designed, nor acid rains that foam and pit whatever they touch. When the globe heats up, and methane steams from the seabed, heating the globe even more, and the seas suffocate (again) till the only survivors are sulphur-eating bacteria, so the biosphere can almost be smelled from space—a huge, blue, putrid egg holding a dying 99 percent of species (and for each, there is a last animal who wanders, calling and calling, and lies down by a bank of turf that, for all its strength to rise, may as well be on the moon)—well! None of that is ordained. Nothing can be concluded except the fact that changing the global climate leads to extinction as night speaks unto night.

Yes, I think of Penelope reweaving her web. But there is no going back to zero, there is no going back, period, even reverses and repetitions are forward momentum, life's rhythm of and-because-and-because, the purest form of history.

And the trilobites, with three hundred million years of heritage, ten orders, one hundred and fifty families, five thousand genera, and twenty thousand species—have perished to the last mouthpart. Prolific even in death, their species are still multiplying in the fossil record, being counted and classified by a strange beast with a skimpy past and uncertain future. The last trilobites are modest, shrunken, like the prints of fingertips. *Requiescant*.

Now the Golden Egg endures a time of supreme trial. It teeters, figuratively, on the narrow, wind-scooped ledge of evolution's dead end. Its numbers plunge. How not, when instead of trilobites that gnawed just so, it has to rely on molar-wielding masticators to spit out its pitlike young, and on constipated sharks? At first, the Golden Egg does what most desperate organisms do: what it used to do. It adjusts the hardness of shells, the action of vents; it courts luck with better conditions for what used to work. With predictable failure. But in time, a mystery flowers: the Golden Egg finds its truth, a truth as unique and necessary as its fair foe, sweet scourge, and dearest dread, the lost trilobites. And not a moment too soon.

Pangea dissolves; ocean beds (again) become cloud-ringed peaks; this earth, not new, not old, thrums under monumental reptiles that mash their chicken tracks into the fossil record. Joy of joys, over conifer forests the maniraptors are aloft! Nine thousand species of birds descend from maniraptor nestlings, their beaks agape, shrilling. Music has evolved in the air. If I had been waiting, I would have been glad I did—though suddenly the sky is dust, ashes, roars, and sandpaper. Under sable clouds, in adamant gloom, the forests rot over the rotting dinosaurs, and for a weird historical moment, terrestrial topography is a Boolean ooze of phosphorescent domes, stalks, fungal shelves, funnels, and wrinkled gills.

Then the ferns grow back as they did in my lifetime on charred Mount Saint Helens. For any age can interpose itself into the calendar of life, if circumstances permit. Any vista can return, any being can reawaken, more or less—the differences are what history is.

The Golden Egg survives the asteroid, alongside newcomers like ducks and regulars like crocodiles; outwardly it appears the same, but inwardly all is changed. Habitat, dry or wet, doesn't matter anymore. Like a sage, it lives by the grace of things beyond the present place and moment. Formerly filled with seawater, it is now filled with semi-heavy water, which, when hit by cosmic rays, emits a burst of cold fusion energy, turned by the Egg's superb bacteria into food. Dinner is served every century or so. Luckily, semi-heavy water, which prolongs the life of fruit flies, works wonders on the simpler organism, allowing it to wait for dinner, and for the withering away of its outer skin—if no animal assists—every forty thousand years. This period is not arbitrary. Like any egg, the Golden Egg needs to be rotated, and though no mother bird turns it with her beak, it has Mother Earth, completing a wobble around her axis every forty millennia. So the Golden Egg's lifecycle matches the tilt of a wandering star. Fortunate beast! It lives at the point of balance among powers: Sol, Earth, bacteria. With boundless energy, it is rich, yet the key to its wealth is balance. Humans can't use natural cold fusion because we demand much more energy—more than we can get without prodding nature into military-grade chain reactions.

That's a problem of balance, not resources: the Golden Egg lives within its means. Yet despite my moralizing on its difference from us, there is a point of closeness, an overlap, where a hand may reach for a Golden Egg, after a last glance at human progress.

Fern forests shrivel, grasslands spread, and over them skim horse-forms faster and faster because a squirrelly tree-leaper grew and grew and now charges their herds in the full cry and majesty of wolfhood. Over grass-foamed savannahs the years blur by until *Equus*, sole surviving horse, running like a tornado on a single, elongated toe, leaps clear into a field of icicles, leaving a glittering chain of hoofprints that do not melt, but meld into a frozen river a mile high in the air. The glacier's rock-hard arm rolls up the forests of Canada like a sleeve and goes to work, seizing North America by its scruff; and in four pulses, changes its grip. At my home address a giant ice talon, clawed with Canadian jaspers, rakes through the stone seabed in one long screech of a million years, leaving, at last, Niagara Falls hissing with rainbows. Solid roads of ice turn cheesy, withdrawing; the gravel spilled into potholes is left, marooned, in mounds, and would you look at this—buried in this mound, here, lies a bit of whelk shell, scraped, scored, and pierced by the agency you are using to hold this page, and I am using to reach, hesitant, toward the Golden Egg. For the polished shell's scratches fit together to make a picture. It depicts an animal, of course. An animal with pricked ears, arched back, and two eyes in its profiled head, both facing you, because the hand doesn't copy what the eye sees, only the idea of what it sees. The idea of a Glacial Kame person was that if an animal had eyes, they were both meant to look at you.

"I see you," says the animal.

THAT WAS ALMOST YESTERDAY, and here I stand today ... thinking about the sybil of Cumae. This prophetess was so old that she dwelt, like a bunch of raisins, in a jar. Her time was spent answering questions that must have been as crushingly repetitious as a march. Will my ships come in? Will I have a child? Should I go to war? Can my sickness be cured? Once, a Roman in the long afternoon of his empire, given to introspection, asked her about herself. Sybil, he asked, what do you want? Her answer was, Death. My palm rests on the scabrous rock, bent fingers casting shadows that could be the bones of a fin, a paw, a wing ... inside, the Golden Egg. Waiting to be cracked. Like the sybil, it is full of the past and future at once. And like the sybil, it knows what is enough.

A lull passes through the insect chorus, except for one voice like the fluttering of an exposed watchspring. There are smells of dried grass and a swampy freshness from the pond, where slimed, peridot rocks crowd the roots of bowing rushes. Okay! Now I have drawn you the picture of an animal. It has no eyes for you, but you can look at it, while I'm off to check my birdhouses.

Rare Invisible Beasts

I

Though I strive to explain the ways of invisible beasts, the Oormz resists all but the most superficial observation. This is poignant because I live with an Oormz and observe it daily. It merits description because of its vital connection to us despite its mysteriousness. My main reason for including the Oormz, though, is one that even scientists equipped with invincible theories, high-powered laboratories, and big data find themselves facing. One must accept that some projects are in the hands of a future generation.

The Oormz

I HAVE AN OORMZ THAT LIVES in the corner of the window behind my desk. In summer, it's ashen blue, like sphagnum moss; in winter, the pale buff of dead leaves. Now, on a cold October day, it's browning around the edges, like the redbud leaves outside the window. It resembles a mohair wrap thrown over the curtain rod. In its brown patches, less fluffy than the blue, I observe the glint of tiny beadlike sensors that lie by the dozens under its nap. Each sensor caps a knotted cluster of the microfibers that make it possible for the Oormz to cling to smooth walls and ceilings, just as a gecko does. A gecko's pads don't work by suction. Instead, they're packed with fine, hairlike fibers that adhere to surfaces through sheer electricity. To break the bond, a gecko curls its toes; the Oormz curls its whole body, and then some.

I can call my Oormz by pursing my lips and making kissing sounds. Trained with saucers of sugar water, it now responds to my signal without a reward, like a dog. Of course, a dog acts from habit and affection—but no one knows what an Oormz feels, or why it does things, or what, precisely, it does. All we know is how they make us feel.

After a few air kisses, I watch it contract like a jellyfish, its center coiling into a bluish misty rosette, while its edges ripple faster and faster into a buff halo. This activity is quite soundless, and no one knows precisely how the Oormz comes afloat over my head, spreading like oil on water, almost as if it were gliding along fault lines in the air. Then it covers my head—I brush it from my face—and drapes its faint cashmere over my shoulders, catching, incorrigibly, in my eyeglass hinge. It smells like damp sawdust or an old willow-bark basket, though when it seems sick, I've known it to smell like stale vegetable oil. Too delicate to stroke (I might injure its sensors,) almost like a coating of bluish brown dust, it nevertheless has a strong, immediate effect. No sooner has it settled than the pressure wedged in my spine and shoulder joints streams away. My shoulders relax into the memory of a fast swim . . . oh, thirty years ago . . .

As I stood up from the lake, swimsuit dragging, my shoulders were bedecked in a crushing robe of gravity under which they squared, while my knees bent like golden hinges, and the new weight I bore only proved a young animal's strength. It comes back to me, *the path through cold sand, cocoa-colored from pine needles*, and I remember what sweetness there was in this old life of mine.

That's what an Oormz does. It's like a bandage between

your animal past, sadly forgotten, and your present. I've known periods dominated by pettifogging human order and base human violence, when my Oormz has restored the memory of kneeling by the first spring I'd ever seen, my lips in the same water containing flowers and emerald moss. I wish everyone had a taste of that, and for that matter, I wish everybody had an Oormz.

What else can I say of this creature, with its nonexistent social life and mysterious biology—this merciful enigma, which now, in clear preference for the window corner, levitates and sidles toward it like a stratus cloud? A few papers quiver and flatten; the air's doing something-or-other. I know no more.

Except an old story. According to a speleological legend, deep under one of North America's large cavern systems lies an enormous chamber, a bubble in the earth's mantle, completely sealed. Inside it, like a woodchuck in a snug burrow, lives an Oormz that is miles long yet no thicker than an earlobe, suspended from the roof and walls. Because of its size, the monster is vulnerable to spreading rips and tears, so nature has given it a marvelous failsafe. Instead of having a heart, lungs, digestive tract, or other organs with specific functions, every one of the Oormz's vessels, from its gossamer capillaries to its yard-wide ducts, performs all its life functions in a complex sequence regulated by valves and pumps, from proton pumps and cell vacuoles to muscle valves—a sequence, mind you, that never repeats itself.

To imagine this, suppose you injected the Oormz with a dye that changed color whenever a vessel changed its function. Red dye would mean circulation; blue, respiration; green, endocrine; purple, immune; orange, sensory— and so on. Moments after your dye diffused through the immense mist of the Oormz, you would be standing with your head thrown back and your eyes trying to crawl out of it. The stained-glass windows of all the human cathedrals multiplied by factors of a thousand, set in motion like a kaleidoscope, without a single buttress, arch, or mullion—without, in the stone heart of the earth, anything to interrupt the miles of animal rainbow—is an image suggesting what you would see.

The story has always struck me in its melancholy tone and fanciful humor. A creature of infinite variety, locked in an unchanging dungeon; a creature that comforts us with animal memories, whose nature we cannot fathom. From whom we can learn the worth of our time, never to be repeated.

2

Can nonhumans feel empathy? The primatologist Frans de Waal adduces many examples. Chimpanzees comfort and pet their peers who have lost fights, and rhesus monkeys refuse to pull a chain that delivers food to them if it causes an electric shock to another rhesus monkey. Nor is empathy confined to primates. Rats liberate other rats from cages before helping themselves to chocolate—an impressive feat, as this chocolate-lover must admit. I'm intrigued by the topic because of the Hypnogator. Without the personal events that made me feel a twinge of empathy for this monstrous beast, I would never have solved the puzzle of its evolution. And I would never have understood the creature who revealed the presence of my successor, the next invisible-beast spotter of the twenty-first century.

The Hypnogator

My sister Evie met her unusual husband, Erik, the hero of this tale, when she was a graduate student in soil biology and he was a technical assistant in a psychology laboratory, a modest position he still holds. A naturalized US citizen, Erik was born in an obscure whaling station in Greenland. He's a big bruiser with a musclebound stoop, who peers with small, worried blue eyes from under shelving flaxen brows. His hands are like bunches of bleached plantains, and tough as nails. He is also shaggy, covered in pale hair like some frost-coated figure out of Norse myth, as if he hadn't been born but was calved off the side of an ice floe. I've always thought there was something feral about him—a fluidity, his joints seem oiled—conjuring a creature neither man, animal, nor spirit, but all three: an apparition in the smokiest corner of a Viking hall, fists filled with icicles and thunderbolts. Despite this he is very sweet; the gentlest man I know, a devoted husband and father, and a vegetarian. His entrance into the family was somewhat bumpy. I still remember my father grumbling to my mother something to the effect that his daughter "was not Fay Wray." My mother countered, in her soothing way, that gorillas made reliable, upstanding mates—not literally upstanding, but he knew what she meant. Then she called Dad "my funny honey monkey," which he didn't seem to appreciate. But we were all glad to have a man in the family after Dad was killed in a laboratory accident involving his work with high-energy particles. (I've promised not to discuss the details, but readers may get a sense of them at the link www.cyriak.co.uk/lhc/lhc-webcams.html.)

Despite our father's misgivings, Evie's marriage transformed her from a thin, pallid, driven girl into a pink-cheeked, exuberantly driven matron, with a double chin the size of her engagement ring's satin cushion. And we discovered Erik's many virtues. He was handy with tools. He enjoyed music. He had a way of stopping sisterly spats by coming between us bodily, searching our faces, a great hand on each upset woman's shoulder; and while we might have resented this in someone else, Erik with his quiet glower seemed to recall us to reason. We felt better for his being among us. He read our favorite periodicals, too—*Nature, Off de Waal Comix,* the *Journal of Irreproducible Results*. And he collected a steady paycheck from the psych lab, where he was evidently prized, with a gift basket of tropical fruit at Christmas. He loved fruit.

Such was the family that encountered the Hypnogator. Evie had invited me to join her, Erik, and their seven-year-old son, Leif, for a few days on a Georgia sea isle, where I would have the chance to see new animals— "visible animals," Evie underlined in that faintly condescending way of hers, as if she really wanted to sigh but had to speak aloud instead.

"You mean babysit while you're at your conference," I replied, deadpan. Bull's-eye!—her next remarks were full of respectful pleading. Leif was such a handful, he adored his Auntie Sophie, et cetera. I had the feeling that if we'd been gorillas, Evie would have been all over my fur, nit-picking in the best sense, then thrusting her infant into my trusty, hairy arms while she scampered away in search of the analogue to scientific exchange. Maybe I wouldn't have gone, for all her verbal grooming, if my Oormz hadn't drifted down from its corner in the window, sifting over my ear, hand, cell phone, and mouth as if on cue. My Oormz is one of those creatures that are invisible to everyone but me; it looks a little like a smoky blue mohair wrap. Today, it smelled of stale vegetable oil and felt a little threadbare. Toto—as I call my Oormz—seemed to hint that we could both use a change of scene. So I agreed, and disembarked one sweltering July morning onto a soggy dock, with a tote bag, full of Toto, over my shoulder.

"Don't tickle," I muttered, as my invisible pet crept up my neck, and the young man unloading my overnight bag shot me a strange look. I smacked Toto and smiled. "I have this habit of talking to mosquitoes."

"Ma'am," he replied, "they don't listen." We trekked

uphill. The place was absolutely strange, a throwback to some musty Zanclean, or Clarkforkian, age of the world. We reached a lawn of sand and tough grass infested with inchling cacti that caught in my sandals. The light was a brilliant gloom, coming down through a webwork of live oaks that loomed very tall and very low, tangling with one another's enormous, twisty branches, from which Spanish moss drizzled in an abandon that made me fearful for Toto—if it flew into one of those trees, I could never tell it apart from the ashen draperies. The shadows at our feet might have been copied from the set of *Nosferatu*, though it was broad daylight, or sweating daylight, for moisture twinkled in the salt air. I was shown to a pleasant room full of ersatz antiques, which reassured and bored at once, a great place to nap. Toto swooped out of the bag and headed for the tufted bedspread where it wriggled contentedly, like a blue Persian cat without the cat attitude or other landmarks. I went out to absorb the scenery before joining my relatives.

A sand trail ringed the island, furrowed by vehicle tires and overgrown by live oaks, moss swags, and palmettos; a jungle tunnel in which wet heat stagnated and my footsteps were muffled. I followed a signpost to "The Beach," which led me to an abrupt vista of yawning, wind-carved dunes, without shade or animal movement, marching away through hostile, glittering air. The sea was a distant, mercury-colored smear, and the whole place breathed slow death. My fantasy of a quick dip shattered, almost audibly. I slogged with sinking spirits back to the inn, passed through the giant live-oak grove, and right over my head, something screamed.

"Jesus!" I yelped, looking up at my nephew Leif, who lay on a limb, flapping his little arms. My hand rose to my lips—what if he fell?

"Raaaark! Raaark!" Leif screamed again, "I'm a velociraptor! Better look out! Auntie Sophie, look! Raaark!"

"Hey," I called. "Come down and give Auntie a kiss." He screeched again, a blond monkey in a sailor jersey and jeans, knees gripping the limb, blue eyes smoky with joy. Prehistoric raptors didn't listen to their aunts. I found Erik lying on the inn's porch swing, his shaggy legs asprawl, reading journals and slowly transferring grapes from a red china bowl into his mouth. Passersby gave him a hard stare when he turned the journal pages with his toes. From Erik, I gathered that Evie rode the island ferry to the mainland after breakfast and didn't return till dinnertime. That set our daily pattern. Erik supervised Leif during the early part of the day while I went hiking. He returned in the afternoon, when I brought my nephew back to my room for a bath and a nap. Then Erik climbed onto the naturalist's jeep for the daily tour, of which he never tired. The naturalist, Sam, a graying expert with an old salt's complexion and unhurried speech, liked Erik. Not so the other guests—at the beverage counter, they splattered iced tea on themselves when Erik's fist swept up sugar packets. They scuttled aside when he ambled through the gift shop, trying on hats. You'd have thought he was a wild animal rather than an easygoing family man. But Erik and Sam were friends, exchanging chuckles, grunts, glints, and meaningful nods. At dinner, Evie, tired from her ferry ride, told us about her day while supplying dialogue for Leif's tabletop skits starring his plastic dinosaurs, Steggy and Rex. For these dramatic parts, Evie doubled up her chin and spoke in a gruff low voice, giving her anecdotes a schizoid quality. The only catch in our arrangements was the stress on Toto. Before his nap, Leif liked to jump on my bed. Like a fledgling, he would soar and plunge, flapping his arms, screeching and singing, while the sensitive Oormz clung to the ceiling and shook.

THE MORNING OF MY DISCOVERY began with a noisy breakfast during which Steggy and Rex fought a battle beside Leif's glass of orange juice, and toppled it twice. While his parents mopped, I sneaked off into the crepitating palmettos. The trail smelled like arboreal body odor, a musk of indescribable antiquity that made my lungs strain to remember their gillhood. The path fell sharply to either side, rising opposite in a shallow bank, where I spotted a ragged hole. I thought it was an alligator hole. That was exciting. I toed down the steep side, hugging red pines, and rubbernecked as far as I dared. Sure enough, in the dark hole, over a gleam of water, lurked two silver, ghostly eyes, staring from behind a bump of nostrils. The rest of the gator was immersed, waiting. Judging from the hole's size, this was a smallish animal, maybe ten feet. I was too big a mouthful: otherwise, it would have submerged, hiding under the water that baited its trap, to conceal its shiny, giveaway eyes. It didn't think me worth catching. But those eyes, fixed on me, gave me chills—and resuming the path, I felt safer. That would have been all, if a rustle hadn't made me look back. An opossum had emerged from the palm scrub, and was trundling toward the gator hole. Marsupial tragedy and crocodilian lunch were imminent. The opossum, a female, waved her snout, sniffing water. Her face was affecting, with its white heart-shaped mask.

"Shoo!" I cried, violating Evie's rule of noninterference with other species. Too bad—I was a mammal chauvinist. "Scat!" She sat, glaring over her furry shoulder. Big ugly human. Then she dismissed me, waving her tight pink nose all around as if tracing fragrant signatures, her paws limp at chest height like a squirrel's. From her belly pouch hung, of all things, a sock ornamented with a turquoise pompon.

"Ha," I breathed. This was no ordinary opossum! She was a Poltergeist Possum, the invisible kind that pilfers human belongings. No wonder she wasn't afraid of humans. People don't kill Poltergeist Possums; they just go on looking for their lost socks or car keys. Now, as I stood on the tire-rutted path, suspicions began to stir. Down inside the dark hole, the alligator had not submerged. Its moonstone eyes were fixed ... on the opossum? No, surely not. The gator couldn't see the invisible opossum. Only invisible beasts can see other invisible beasts, as a rule. It just happened to be looking in her direction ... but so fixedly? I sat slowly on my haunches, suspense cracking in every joint. If those shiny optics vanished and the nostrils sank, it could mean that I had discovered an invisible alligator ...

Then the unaccountable happened. The opossum gaped, her tooth-tips like ivory pencil points, and growled at the hole. That made no sense. Why was she growling? If threatened she ought to flee, or play dead. The shiny eyes blinked. Left, right, left, right ... Why was the alligator blinking? Was I dreaming? I shook my head; my thoughts turned misty and scattered as I watched the opossum, with erratic growls, trailed by her ratty tail and turquoise pompon, lurch the rest of the way down the dirt track and—horrible—flail out of sight, under the rocking, glinting water's surface, with a muted splash. Another splash, a headless blob flung about, water again, an armor-ridged spine ... Jesus Christ, I thought dimly, I have got to ... I have got to ... before I completed the thought, my feet had covered the mile back to the inn. When I tottered up the porch steps, I ran into the Erik and Sam, mulling over a digital camera, checking out its features. They treated me like an emergency.

"Drink," Sam declared, tearing the cap off a water bottle. Erik loomed very tall and grimaced, with clenched fists, in the direction I had come. His polo shirt swelled; his icy brows bristled. Whatever was out there had better leave his sister-in-law alone. Between the two of them,

I felt much better. I said I'd seen a possum nabbed by a gator and asked Sam to have another look at the hole, which he checked every day and believed to be deserted. The two men zipped off in the jeep, only to return shrugging their shoulders. Any sign Sam knew of, of gators, was not there, but he promised to keep an eye on it; the word *eye* gave me chills.

Thus I proved that my alligator was invisible: it could see an invisible opossum, but humans could not see it. The next day, Leif grew bored with velociraptors.

It was inevitable.

Near the inn, on its cactus-infested lawn, lay a sunken cement enclosure that was once a fountain's basin, and all day, guests loitered there viewing a pair of young alligators with jagged smiles. They were four feet long and glowed like lava. At our second dinner together, in the evening, Evie told her little boy that the two alligators were *living dinosaurs*. We all laughed, watching the potato on the end of Leif's fork stop in his open mouth, right under his round, shining eyes.

"That's right," Evie said. "Eat your potato. So, you want Mommy to tell you about the gators?" Leif chewed, nodding so violently that Erik performed a calming pass over his son's head, and began transferring forkfuls of carrots into the little face hidden behind his great snowy hand. I watched our candlelit reflection in the French windows; Erik's unevenly slouched back was Mont Blanc, Evie's sharp, sunburnt face was an explorer's. The longer she talked, the more inferior

I felt. I had no solar panel scales on my back, no special palate to open my mouth underwater and continue breathing through my nose above water, no moveable lungs to enhance maneuverability. No bone-digesting stomach full of gastroliths. I could run on two legs? Oh. Alligators ran thirty miles per hour on land. Alligators hydroplaned across water, too. Oh, and survived underwater without breathing for several hours by rerouting their circulation. What was I? What was humanity? Sam entered the dining room; the naturalist caught my eye in the window and made a gesture I liked, something between tipping a hat and showing a palmed card. I pushed back my chair and said good night, busy day tomorrow, not mentioning that my business was with an invisible alligator.

The next day, I hiked out eagerly, with questions. Did my gator hide its shiny eyes underwater even when its prey couldn't see it? In other words, did it behave like a visible alligator, or was its behavior modified by invisibility? Another morning's observation gave me the answer. My gator did not hide its eyes underwater. Like their visible cousins, invisible gators are stealth hunters, but evolution has given them a supreme advantage that makes most stealthy behaviors redundant. My gator submerged only when the prey was caught, to speed its death by drowning. Most of its prey would be visible—yesterday's Poltergeist Possum, poor thing, was exceptional. I still didn't understand why she hadn't fled the spot.

Now, I have to admit that although I try to love all

creatures, my alligator was uphill work. Think of being slammed between those jaws, impaled on eighty teeth, water exploding into your lungs as you're ripped and shaken into bloody gobbets. Was this a beast, or a torture chamber with a mind? I must admit, shamefully, to some hatred. The hardest moment involved baby raccoons. Young raccoons don't desert their siblings. That's why raccoon roadkill often comes in twos: the second one has failed to abandon its dead brother or sister in passing traffic. I should have been consoled by the knowledge that raccoons will cheerfully eat baby alligators. But I wasn't.

The first little raccoon—a sooty-faced, ring-tailed puffball—at first scooted free of the water hole and yelled for help as only a raccoon can yell, like a siren being ground in a disposal. My hamstrings yanked and I might have lost my head (or other limbs) racing to its rescue, if a scaly, dripping, blunt snout hadn't shot out of the hole and whisked back underwater, as an infant yell etched itself through the insensate forest. Minutes died away. Then along came the second little raccoon, Bro or Sis, its potato-sized body vibrating over soft black fingers splayed in the dirt. It chattered like a manual alarm clock being wound, a percussive clucking purr. It searched, argued with itself, searched some more, looked at the sky, nodded back and forth before the gator hole, sniffed in the dirt, went round in a trembling circuit, and seemed at a loss. Meanwhile, two cold moonstones shone in the lair, without any expression a mammal could read. I dabbed at the tears behind my binoculars. To hell with research: I threw stones and shouted to scare off the little raccoon, but as it retreated, the striped palmetto leaves gave away its position in the brush. It didn't go far. After I'd straightened up and painfully regained the path, aching in various body and soul parts, the little raccoon probably renewed its search. I didn't want to know.

That afternoon I looked for Leif, but instead ran into Sam on the inn's porch.

"Leif's got the gator bug," Sam informed me, pulling items from his various pockets—a penlight, a calculator, a tube of antibiotic, a chocolate bar—and rearranging them into other pockets. "He's gone to look at them. I was just heading down there." He beckoned, circling with his arm, the way a big dog looks around and dips his head in a circle, for you to follow. I liked Sam—nothing seemed to bother him much, except for the misuse of national parklands. We strolled through the moist sunshine to the spot where my nephew lay, beside the fenced enclosure. What made a little boy go belly-down on concrete, propped on his elbows, sneakers butterflied to left and right, showing us the crabapples of his tonsils?

"Leif, what are you doing?" Leif's mouth was a clear pink O rimmed with milk teeth. "Leif, aren't you going to tell me?" I knelt beside him and tweaked his nose. He bit my hand. "Hey!"

"I'm gaping," he explained with dignity. "Gators gape to cool off."

"Maybe," Sam demurred. "We don't really know why they do that." Leif gaped again and I found I had to yawn. "Now I'm gonna yawn," said Sam and did. "Yawns are infectious and so is scratching. That's primate behavior, monkey see, monkey do. Tell you what, Leif—when a monkey sees another monkey grab something, the same cells light up in his brain as if he grabbed it himself, did you know that? Primates are hardwired to imitate others. We pick up the feelings of others by imitation, too. That's called empathy." He pitched his voice for my ear. "Women are supposed to be better at it than men." I glanced up and felt my body send a telegram—and looked hastily down again.

Leif snapped his jaws, turned red, and bawled through his tears, "Ow, my tongue! Auntie Sopheeee! I bit my tongue and it huuuurts!" I hugged Leif with more than due diligence while Sam assumed a stance of scientific detachment, hands in pockets, and watched the alligators gape, their creamy throats working below immobile, open jaws.

THAT NIGHT, I FRETTED and tossed, tugged one way by an impression that if I got close to Sam he would smell like warm sand, and the other way by the need to spend my time wisely. How many invisible alligators would I have the chance to observe, back home, versus how many human males? And supposing Sam were unique, a heartfind, what good would it do when he discovered that my house, my car, all my activities, were arranged around invisible beasts? Sam was a devoted naturalist. He lived in a parallel, nonintersecting universe, waiting for a woman who loved visible nature as much as he did. But I tossed and turned, until Toto disengaged from my pillow and plastered itself to the ceiling. Humans love drama. An Oormz wants peace.

We had two days left on the island, and I spent the morning behind binoculars, crouched in the scrub, my note-pad on one knee. Rain had stormed through the night, and the ground before the gator hole had liquefied into clay-red puddles, reflecting palmetto fronds. They looked like blades in blood. My gator was having a slow day, since the island's animals were drinking rainfall. I had to search for its black nostrils, their rims exactly even with the water. This tactic spelled hunger. A gator's head is covered with sen-sors that detect the slightest shimmy of the water's surface; clearly, my gator was maximizing its sensor use. The twin eyes looked a little bleary, I thought. Of course an alligator wouldn't mind lying in water up to its eyelids, for hours, for a meal, would it? By noon it had caught nothing, while cricket frogs visited the puddles like muddy raindrops. To a ten-foot-long reptile, they meant about as much as a sprin-kling of jimmies to a hungry man—and in any case, they weren't jumping into the lair. They were just rubbing it in.

I went back for lunch and looked for my family. Erik wasn't on the porch swing. I strode over the lawn, calling for Leif, and heard my name shouted by a chef at the kitchen entrance, a spike-haired youth in a white apron, calling through cupped hands; and when I pelted up he repeated that Leif had been missing since early morning and a search party had gone out, in Sam's jeep. He apologized for hollering at me, and the kitchen crew gathered, flour paste on their fronts, sweat on their hairlines. I thanked everybody, then went and stood still under the live oaks as pure alarm drained down my muscles and out my soles. Obsession ran in our family. Leif had the gator bug. The missing factor in the equation came to me, the thing my body was trying to tell me. It was what Leif had said, yesterday, when I'd tucked him in for his nap.

"Auntie Sophie," he'd asked, "could a gator eat a velociraptor?"

"Nope." But his eyebrows drew together in a miniature version of his father's bristling shelves.

"Could a gator come in a house?" I'd stroked his cheek.

"Nope. We have special alligator alarms that go off, special alligator barriers, electronic barriers that keep them out." My nephew flung himself on his back and stared at the ceiling.

"Where's the alarm? Is it on the ceiling?"

"It's invisible. The technology is invisible so it won't spoil the pretty rooms. Now go to sleep," I'd said firmly, and went into the bathroom to put on my makeup for dinner. Leif was murmuring to himself; I'd been pleased that he was finally drifting off. Now I heard the words that I'd ignored. Leif had murmured, "Safe . . . on the ceiling . . . nice velociraptor."

It wasn't nonsense, after all. *Leif had been reassuring Toto, a creature on the ceiling, who reminded him of a velociraptor.* That could only mean one thing. My nephew could see invisible beasts. And for the last two evenings, over dinner, he'd heard the adults chaffing Aunt Sophie about the alligator she thought she'd seen on the trail. And alligators were Leif's passion, his obsession, and I began to move toward the forest as a runner heads into a collapsing tunnel . . .

AFTER WHAT I WITNESSED and experienced at the alligator lair, sleep was out of the question. That night, sleep was a quaint custom belonging to a remote era. I seized a candlestick, wrapped myself in a terry-cloth robe, and crept down four flights, passing closed doors, hearing snores, feeling the wooden weight of the early hours, rubbing my palm over the round banister finial at each landing to make sure I was awake. My candle flickered. I paused until it regained its composure. The inn, at this hour, felt like the backstage of something, a dream maybe, in which a person without gender or identifying complexities drifts, vaguely lit, toward no known end. I froze before crossing the ray that shone from underneath the door to Evie and Erik's room. My sister and her husband were awake, and no wonder. They surely had much to discuss.

I skated on my toes past that tense ray, and finally, with

a sense of dubious triumph, stood in the parlor before the leather armchair where I'd promised myself, a long time ago and several flights up, to spend the wee hours thinking. I set the candle on a mahogany table corner, which it glorified, and got into the armchair, which had unforeseen bumps and angles. But it was good. My thinking, however, was swamped by frog song, the loudest, highest, densest, most vibrant frog song in the universe at that hour. Gradually I grew used to the smudges around the room, reminiscent of their daylight shapes, lyrebacked chairs and ball-footed tables, and the glimmer of windows whose drapes were pinned back to admit the intangible glow of night clouds. Then there was a shadow moving toward me on human feet.

"Hello," said a voice. Someone bent over me and rested two long, reddened, creased hands on the ends of my armrests. I raised the candle to see, from underneath, its slightly alarming synopsis of Sam's face. We talked in near whispers. He'd seen my light from outside; he kept late hours.

"Usually if I see a light, it's kids getting up to trouble. I'm glad it's you," he said, and paused. "It was kind of rough, out there at the gator hole. I don't mind fixing a drink, if you'd care for one. Help you sleep," he added, conscientiously. So Sam fixed us gin and tonics, working with a flashlight and surprisingly few clinks and clatters. Our glasses touched in the candlelight; Sam sat in a twin armchair, on the other side of the illuminated table. We couldn't see each other, but it didn't matter. He wanted me to explain things he didn't understand about the gator hole *affaire*. I tried, flushed with alcoholic frankness, but it was difficult. You don't keep a secret like invisible beasts your whole life, and then casually confess to the first gin-slinging naturalist who comes along. Also my memories were so muddled that Sam tried to straighten them out with his own version.

"When Erik and I drove up," he commenced, "there you were on all fours, clutching the boy and yelling, and he looked like he was trying to crawl away from you, and you were both covered in mud." He paused. "It sounds funny now, but at the time you sounded—I'm sorry, but you sounded like the devil was after you. I honked the horn but you went right on yelling and trying to hold on to Leif. Then your brother-in-law jumped out of the jeep and pulled up a tree. Never seen anything like it. He pulled up a pine sapling and flung it at the gator hole. And he was whooping and hollering like a—well. Remember that?"

"I don't remember anything till I, sort of came to, in the jeep. I'm sorry I was acting so crazy." Sam laughed slightly.

"There's another thing—how you got in the jeep. Erik slung you under one arm, and the kid under the other, like it was nothing. Threw you both in together. Never saw such a guy. Was he ever in pro wrestling? I don't mean to pry. Look," Sam urged, in a low voice, "I've really enjoyed meeting you, Sophie, and your folks. I'm just a bit puzzled what to make of you all." I stretched my feet into the darkness, toed the leather piping on the footrest, sighed, and said, "We were hypnotized. Leif and I."

"Hypnotized? By what?"

"By the alligator. No, listen. It had strange eyes. It blinked in a strange way—"

"*Bli-inked?*" Southern incredulity. I tried again. I shut my eyes and did my best to describe the awful picture behind them. It was why I'd given up sleep: when I shut my eyes, the cold, ugly, glowing stones appeared. They blinked, left, left, right, I couldn't stop my mind from following their code, the code to confusion. I remembered that I'd locked onto Leif's kicking body, but a mental mist—like the one when you're about to black out—had kept me from knowing, except in glimpses, if I was still holding on, or if my nephew was gone, crawling to that dreadful pool, summoned. There wasn't even an "I"—just a mosaic of terrors and struggles, the precious glimpses of Leif still with me, still kicking, trying to crawl toward the monster; and through it all those damned eyes, drilling away, blink by blink. Left right right left. Trying to convey this to Sam, I lost courage and drained my glass; it occurred to me that I looked drunk and red-nosed, in a bathrobe, and was grateful for the dark, and for the frogs' singing as the words stumbled out. Sam uttered a soft snort. And the frogs kept singing.

"Tell you what," Sam said at last, "I hear a lot of ghost stories, on this island. Elf lights. One summer it was all elf lights. Some family had left their dog toys behind, those balls that glow in the dark? Don't be mad at me because that's not what I think your story is. I don't think so because I did some poking around. I've seen tracks, which proves nothing because gators move around; could be any gator's tracks. But I also found cached prey, stuck in the roots right beside that hole—"

"A baby raccoon." I sniffled into a cocktail napkin. "I saw it die."

"Yes, that's right," Sam said slowly. "There are clear signs of a gator in that hole. You got lucky, seeing him, or unlucky, and maybe he wouldn't have scared you so much if your nephew hadn't tried to get friendly with him. That would scare anybody. Fear does strange things. If you say the animal blinked, well, maybe he did, but there's always a reason for these things. His eyes may be injured." Suddenly I wanted to look at Sam, not his shadow. I took the candle and slid forward to hold the small light nearer to that voice in the dark. To my surprise, Sam was leaning forward too, elbows on knees, and I startled, having expected air where his face was blooming out, his brow grooved deeply above the smiling eyes. "Don't you feel a little sorry for the fellow, Sophie? Having some sort of, what, ocular discomfort, and no doctor around?" This point of view, the squinting Hypnogator's, hadn't occurred to me, but it did now with an odd soft intensity. I thought about it. Sam's fingers were laced; the heels of his palms met and parted, met and parted like a question—trust her, don't trust her? I put my hand in his. After that, there was nothing but to go upstairs together.

That night, Sam showed me how alligators make love. It wasn't toothy. They slide against each other, slowly, to their full length. We did a lot of muffled laughing. When I fell asleep, I saw my alligator sliding through the salt marsh, and beside him another, a female, gliding along. Their two armored noses just cleared the water in the moonlight, crisscrossed by sighing rushes. Then I started to laugh in my dream, because instead of cold, hypnotic eyes, I saw two pairs of tortoiseshell eyeglasses, one with rhinestone corners, perched on those saurian snouts! What happens to their glasses when the gators dive?—I wondered and awoke. The bed was covered in moonlight. I spread my fingers in it, and lightly patted the blankets mounded over Sam. The explanation for the alligator's behavior spilled out of my dream and into thought.

My alligator was nearsighted! It squinted and blinked because it was trying to see. At some point in the past eighty million years or so, evolution began to favor invisible alligators who squinted in a particular pattern that had the effect of hypnotizing—not visible prey, who couldn't see its shiny eyes—but invisible prey, who could. My gator probably didn't realize its effect on invisible creatures like that poor Poltergeist Possum: it just squinted at them, perplexed, trying to see why they didn't come closer to its water hole. Not diabolical: myopic! I hugged myself with glee. A gator hypnotist! I dubbed it the Hypnogator. I whispered its name in the moonlight, which had a swim-ming feel, as if it flowed from the dream marshes. Impos-sible to share this with Sam, but something told me that without our night together, I would never have solved the mystery. I slid back under the blankets and into warmth, double-personed, magical; and with it the thought that all rare creatures were happy accidents, and that included the Hypnogator, myself, my Oormz, my Oormz-seeing nephew, my valiant brother-in-law, my indomitable baby sister ... and my lover, fellow-being, this curled, radiant person whose rough toes I found with my own. There. Who could not love a process that refined raw accidents into rare advantages? Evolution was luck in slow motion, luck abiding by purely formal rules that lent it the helpless beauty of swan songs and the energy of good jokes. Per-haps, if Sam could understand as much as that, I'd find a way to tell him more. And I listened to the tree frogs keep on singing, wave after wave of them, perpetually on key.

3

Nothing is more American than the study of butterflies. We proudly number many butterfly savants in our history, like Samuel Scudder, chronicler of the monarch. Indeed, our Declaration of Independence says that happiness is to be pursued, as one chases butterflies with nets. As a patriotic citizen, I duly add this note concerning invisible butterflies.

Grand Tour Butterflies

I CALL THE INVISIBLE BUTTERFLIES "Grand Tours" because of their extensive travels. Monarch butterflies travel three thousand miles in their brief, nine-month lives, but invisible butterflies outdistance them. There are three varieties, of which one is the rarest. You cannot chase it. Once, it chased me—scared the daylights out of me, too, though I adored every minute. That's how unusual it is. Each variety of Grand Tour defends itself with its wing display, designed to discourage predators (that is, invisible predators, which can see Grand Tours, and are quite as deadly as their more conspicuous counterparts). This is hard to do, because very few animals—whether frogs, mantises, spiders, snakes, wasps, rats, ants, or birds—would not like to eat a tasty, helpless butterfly. Of the three Grand Tour varieties, only one really succeeds in defending itself well; that is the one I can't catch. The one that came after me. Here they are, in order of their wing patterns.

1. Aposematically patterned

These Grand Tours are globe-trotters. They travel in search of food and they're not picky; liquefied yak dung or Nile mud slurry are fine. They don't starve, but they do get tired. When thousands of them subside all at once onto a single North American lilac bush, that's a good time to come creeping up behind the bush, brandishing a net. Some will be picking their way, like women in stiletto heels, over lilac clusters to nose into a blossom. But others will be sunning, spreading their wings. And what do the wings of Grand Tours display? Travel pictures. On one wing appears a tan thumbprint; looking closer, you'll see a deserted limestone amphitheater in the glare of noon. Another shows on each wing a steep forest, and on the thorax between them a blue river, and reflected in the river, a brass-colored train climbing deeper and deeper into the sky, among snow-covered Alps. Another shows moonlit sand dunes, pocked with thousands of rust-colored meteors, each in its own sickle of shadow, that have fallen over the course of eons and never been viewed by a human eye. How lucky you are that Grand Tours fly over the Sahara and then perch on your lilacs.

You can thank their unusual scaling. All butterflies have scales consisting of the flat, hard ends of tiny fibers, arranged like a mosaic. On Grand Tours, instead of a flat mosaic, the fiber ends stack up in a three-dimensional pattern, much like the patterns that produce the 3-D image in the corner of your credit card. Grand Tours, essentially, are flying holograms. This variety depends on aposematic patterning, i.e., colorful patterns that warn predators away. Most butterflies' colors tell the predator, "You can't eat me because I taste awful, may be poisonous, and you're really not that desperate." The Grand Tour's travel pictures tell predators, "You can't eat me because I'm far away in a foreign country."

But when you're in big trouble, pretending that you're not really here fools nobody. It's a feeble defense. Most of this type gets eaten.

2. *Aposematically patterned crepuscular*

The crepuscular Grand Tours are seen toward dusk on flowers that stay open all night, like peonies. They have pictures of the universe on their wings, and you can easily spot them if you know a little astronomy. On one pair of black wings, tawny veins depict the brown, boiling dust pillars out of which stars form. Another butterfly exhibits spiral galaxies, one per wing, colliding like squashed, vaporous Ionic capitals. Another is spotted with planets crowned with electric auroras. An uncommon variety, harder to spot in the dimness, shows concentric bands of molecular sludge sloshing away from a diabolical black hole, located on the dorsal abdomen. These planetarium-like displays are perfectly natural; corals and snails also resemble gaseous formations and spiral galaxies, because nature's physical laws tend to multitask her forms. The defense of the crepuscular Grand Tour butterfly lies in telling the predator, "You can't eat me because I'm in outer space."

This merely makes the predator bemused. It prevents nothing, and isn't a good defense.

3. Cryptically patterned chimerical

Crypsis is camouflage. These Grand Tours made a single summer memorable; since then, I have not seen them—though that might point more to my gullibility than to their absence. They use a social defense by swarming together to produce camouflaging illusions, composed, like jigsaw puzzles, out of many individual butterflies. One of their illusions tells a predator, "You can't eat us because we're just a big rock." I was a victim of this trick. One warm day in July, I brought a book and a cold beer up to my pond, to sit on a boulder in the shadiest spot overlooking the water. I was about to set the beer bottle, nicely sweated, by my feet, as I pressed the book open with my thumb and lowered my backside onto a boulder. It was a big, sun-warmed, striated boulder, complete with lichen. Or so it seemed. I fell in the pond, bumped against a bass, and came up snorting water out of my sinuses while my book drowned, and the rocky bank foamed with good Belgian beer, attracting ants, bees, and wasps precisely where I had to scramble up. Around my head danced—as if in mocking solicitude—a cloud of Grand Tours flashing partial images of weathered striations and lichen. Since then I've been as cautious as a dog about where I seat myself. But it was a fair price to pay for seeing the Grand Tours mount a social defense, using the excellent principle of strength in numbers.

The reason I call this variety "chimerical," however, has to do with their most striking use of the social defense, by which, once, I was rendered stupid with astonishment. And if they can do that to a *Homo sapiens*, they can probably stupefy smarter animals too. You might call it the jaw-dropping defense—makes biting much harder for predators . . .

This defense consists of the Grand Tours massing together in the shape of large, fabulous creatures, too big and too weird to tangle with. On a normal spring afternoon, as you leaf through junk mail before entering the house, you hear a stir overhead, and looking up, you stagger backward onto the porch and collapse against the front door, feeling behind your back for the latch with a nerveless hand from which the junk mail has dropped. A snow-white stallion is charging down your yard at the level of the treetops, in the air. On its back, seated between its sky-blue wings, leans a knight. He is clad in armor so bright it sizzles your retinas. He is aiming his lance straight at you. You are numb with fright, flabbergasted, and singing loudly—no, that comes afterward, after a few drinks. Right now, your jaw is dropping at the sight of the stallion's streaming white mane—and the violently lashing lion's tale that sprouts from its equine rump. You can almost hear the butterflies bellowing, "Take that, frogs, mantises, spiders, snakes, wasps, rats, ants, and birds. Take that, you bastards!" You slump onto your threshold, cross your arms over your knees, and give a deep, deep sigh.

It's the best defense. Take courage from this. Nothing beats imagination on the wing.

Invisible Beasts in Print

I

The command of symbolic language is what divides humanity from other animals—so goes the common idea, to which there is some truth. But from the sheep whose tanned hides became the bearers of inked words, to the symbols organizing our thoughts today, other species loom large in language. None more so than Think Monkey.

Think Monkey

SOME BEASTS ARE GOOD TO EAT, some are good to live with, but all are indispensable for thinking with. We think about ourselves with the help of other animals—we are mulish, catty, busy as bees, cold fish, small fry, dogs in the manger, doves, hawks, bearish, bullish, sheepish, cowed, elephantine; we ferret or worm things out; we horse around, clam up, get crabby; some of us are paid moles, and I, personally, am a real bitch. Lacking a beast that precisely suits the purpose, sometimes we have to invent one. Such is Think Monkey.

Think Monkey is the reason why we are not conscious of our inmost thoughts; and why genius, as a poet said, is a secret to itself. She is known to neuroscience by the name of *homunculus*, or "little person." I have reason to believe she is a ho-monkey-lus, or more concisely, Think Monkey.

Hey!—you might object—I *am* conscious of my inmost thoughts.

Well, no. Think it over. Am I conscious of my basic sensory activity, even? Do I feel a hundred billion calcium concentrations dropping inside my neurons, a hundred million sparks merging in wave fronts? No. What I get, as a result of all that frantic activity, is a banana. My banana is yellow and freckled, smells terrific, tastes the way I remember from my last banana, and that's what I'm conscious of. My conscious mind is a representation of the brain's activity. This representation exists so that I can handle the unexpected, which always comes along to threaten a lifeform. Handling the unexpected is what nerve cells doing automatic processing jobs can't do. They can't reflect on what they're doing. But I, being conscious, can.

I can do all sorts of things with my beautiful conscious mind: I can deliberately tear off two more bananas and juggle them—well, no, I can't juggle them. But it was a conscious act while it lasted. Now, these notions passing through my mind are not my inmost thoughts. Those are inaccessible to my conscious mind. My inmost thoughts are massive computations performed by gelatinous giant molecules like alien spaceships bumping and docking and linking with other kinky, slobbery, organic molecules, inside billions of neurons, all of them simultaneously hammering at trillions of specialized, cross-indexed, and crisscross-indexed, and you'll-never-live-through-it-indexed, sorts of jobs. That, thankfully, is not what I'm conscious of when I think.

I am conscious of my self. I can sit here humming *cogito ergo sum* and peeling this yellow, ripe banana, enjoying the creamy ribbed texture where the peel strips off, *mmm*

... and when I've taken a resilient, not mushy, first bite, I consciously look forward to seeing whether the banana's cross-section shows the lucky brown Y or the unlucky three brown dots because I am superstitious... Oh, I do love my banana thoughts! Three cheers for the representation! That's what it is, you know. I am not conscious of my inmost thoughts—and who the hell wants to be? Slimy neurons, yech. Computational functions, brrr. I experience a glorious representation of my inmost thoughts. I experience this—

BANANA!

Anyway.

Now, somebody, some agency or other, must be arranging and taking care of my inmost thoughts, since I certainly can't, I'm totally in the dark about them. Some agency certainly operates my frontal lobe which is responsible for various higher—or more frontal—mental functions. That agency is Think Monkey. Here's what the brain scientists say about her:

> ... *somewhere in the confines of the frontal lobe are neuronal networks that act to all intents and purposes like a homunculus. This is a non-conscious homunculus ... Our homunculus acts more like a computational entity ... it is responsible for many complex operations, such as thoughts, concept formations, intentions, and so on ...* [*]

---

[*] *The Quest for Consciousness: A Neurobiological Approach,* Christof Koch, (Geenwood Village, CO: Roberts & Company Publishers, 2004) p. 298.

Think Monkey creates my intentions, my concepts, and all the treasures of my human intellect. Now, don't go objecting that Think Monkey has to have its own Think Monkey, because as the scientist says, Think Monkey is not conscious, so does not require a counterpart. Think Monkey makes thoughts, but does not think. My Think Monkey sleeps, while her dark clever fingers, toes, and prehensile tail operate, at frantic speed, the jungle-cockpit of neuronal computations. She does everything in a sleep that lasts my whole life long. Not even death will wake her; death, least of all. It seems so unfair. Poor Think Monkey! For an entire lifetime she performs such important work, round the clock, without once being able to reflect and say to herself, "I adore bananas."

Maybe I'll have another one, just in case.

As I said earlier, Think Monkey has no conscious thoughts: she only makes conscious thoughts, but—paradoxically—she makes conscious thoughts about herself. This is one of the spookier aspects of a human mind. I once read a haunting story about an animal researcher who studied cotton-top tamarin monkeys, a cute species the size of squirrels, with amber-eyed, squashed, grave little mugs, feverish hands, and fluffy white manes. One female tamarin liked the researcher very much, and always cooed at him. We don't know why. Sometimes that worried him. One night, he dreamed that his little friend skipped over and offered him, in her needling fingers, a book. It was a clothbound textbook, titled *Dictionary of the Tamarin Language*. This was the Holy Grail of his research—a key to primate communication!—so he was very happy to see it. But when he opened it, it was blank.

Think Monkey, the sleeping simian in our brains who performs our higher mental functions, is also responsible for our dreams. It's a strange thing to imagine. Think Monkey, in her dreamless sleep, without a flicker of consciousness, like a shut-eyed Buddha enthroned among a billion exploding lotus blossoms and lilies of perception and computation, sends down to us a dream, through the long, weird chute that travels between the actual inaccessible and the conscious (although slumbering) mind. People used to think that gods visited them in dreams, taking the form of their lost friends or loves to get their attention, saying: *Gather your maidservants and wash the laundry in the river,* or, *Sacrifice a snow-white bull immediately.* It would have been blasphemy to suggest that these dear ones, so precious to dreaming eyes, were the handiwork of a monkey perched inside the brain. But in Think Monkey's sleep, our thinking is woven, and when its representation comes in dream images, we had better pay attention.

The animal researcher's dream tells the most intimate of truths. Think Monkey—i.e., his conceptual process—weighed his knowledge of cotton-top tamarins and communication, and made a prediction: he would write a book. But Think Monkey also weighed the concept of consciousness itself, which was inevitably part of this researcher's questions. And in answer, Think Monkey sent an image of *herself*: a monkey holding up a blank dictionary—a representation of the very fact that she has nothing to say. Only our conscious minds speak, though our thoughts come straight from the monkey's hands. I can think of no more eerie paradox . . . rather, my Think Monkey can create no more eerie paradox, for me to become conscious of, and speak of . . .

No image captures more surely the intermediate place of our conscious minds, looking around with wonderment between the superb blank of our inmost thought activity, and the stupendous blank of our sensory activity. Is there anything quite like the amazing and paradoxical Think Monkey?

There is. The neuroscientist whom I quoted in the last section yearns for new experiments. Neuroscience is so new! Great discoveries await the experimenter who can decode the chattering of a hundred thousand neurons instead of the few used in most experiments. He urges more experimentation on animals in a duly humane manner, using modern anesthetic technology that

> *permits the monkey to be rapidly and reversibly put to sleep while the electrode stays in place.**

---

* Koch, p. 312.

I can see them now, all those sleeping primates: the limp chimps and conked-out macaques, the gibbons' faces fringed in pale fur like ash-encircled coals. All our cousins getting their beauty sleep, sprouting electrodes for our benefit. A bit pathetic, a bit clownish—but mostly eerie, because Think Monkey's functions also include human creativity. We know that the creative thought process is hidden from the conscious mind. Genius is a secret to itself. Out of nowhere, an idea pops into your head, or makes you sit bolt upright at four in the morning. The procedure that evolved it is hidden; that's the monkey's job. Think Monkey, the universal Muse, creates the flash in which a scientist sees the light. So it is at her prompting that we fill our laboratories with unconscious primates, the living images of Think Monkey herself, as we struggle to fulfill that darkly humorous imperative, Know Thyself.

2

B ecause of Fine-Print Rotifers, I used to believe in going paperless—in creating and storing all documents digitally. Then I learned Silicon Valley's best-kept secret, namely, that the bugs, viruses, and worms infesting the Web are by no means as metaphorical as one tends to assume . . . but that's another story.

Fine-Print Rotifers

FINE PRINT IS HARD TO READ not only because of its painful smallness and dry subject matter. It is also the grazing ground of Fine-Print Rotifers. These microscopic animals are highly destructive. Had humanity never developed ink, then the FPRs, as I'll call them, would not have become pandemic; they would have remained a minor symbiont in plants, and the United States might never have reaped the grim results of the securitization of mortgages. As it is, a plague of protozoa thrives on our need to spell out everything in writing.

Lignin, the most abundant organic material on earth, comes from plants and contains pigments. We see these pigments in paper as it yellows over time. Plants use pigments for many purposes. But since too much of a good thing is always a bad thing, FPRs make themselves useful by ridding plants of surplus lignin pigments. They also kill harmful bacteria—in effect, marinating and cooking them. It is a simple life but elegantly arranged.

Rotifers, under magnification, look like wiggly electric

razors: they have one or two hairy, wheel-shaped organs that whirl food into their gullets. Imagine a wheel hung with fishing lines over a barrel full of fish. An FPR's wheel-hairs act just like that, hooking "fish"—tasty pigment molecules—which they yank off the lignin and drop into the rotifer's gullet, neat and sweet, and I'm sparing you much technical detail. As a by-product, FPRs also excrete a mild acid that softens up bacteria, as a marinade tenderizes meat, and, being slightly heated, cooks them as well. In their natural home on a plant, the rotifers wriggle along cooking and gobbling up any bacteria in their way, while they munch lignin pigments. I suspect that the pigment is a cherished condiment, and FPRs are eaters of the type who upend a bottle of mustard or ranch dressing over everything, and will even guzzle their favorite sauce unaccompanied, like those of us who privately eat maple syrup with a spoon. Be that as it may, plants and FPRs together are the picture of a perfect symbiosis . . . but paper and ink change everything.

Paper contains FPR spores, in the lignin. FPRs hibernate through hard times in spore form, reemerging when they sense the presence of plenty. As soon as ink hits the paper—zap! Invisible rotifers are all over every serif. The abundance of scrumptious pigment drives them wild with appetite, for synthetic ink is vastly more concentrated than lignin pigment—it's like fudge, sirloin steak, and triple crème Brie rolled into one. I don't use the word *swarm*, however, since the rotifers don't move in loose swarms. Far from it. The most spectacular trait of this species is the deliberate route it takes while feeding—in other words, its foraging route.

WE ARE TALKING OPTIMAL foraging theory, which applies to all animal foraging, including your own shopping route. For instance: if you can't buy all your groceries at one store, you try to figure out the most efficient route between stores. This is your foraging route. All predators have one, because for most predators, the stores they patronize try to run away and hide. Think about it. What if you never knew which store would be open, or when? You would search your past experiences for the most common open times, and create a route based on that. Your route would take the shape of the optimal supply of open grocery stores. And where do FPRs find their tasty ink molecules? In letters and words. *So they develop foraging routes in the shapes of letters and words.*

THIS IS HOW AN INNOCENT BEAST causes us misery in varying degrees from the nagging to the catastrophic. Not because the rotifers strip the ink off paper—though they do—but because, at the same time that FPRs remove the original printed words, they also wriggle over the paper in their foraging routes, excreting a mild acid, slightly heated, as mentioned. Now, it just so happens that putting mild acid on paper, and then heating it, is the classic recipe for invisible ink. You can easily imitate the foraging routes of FPRs yourself. Just write a few words using lemon juice for ink, then heat the paper you've written on. Gradually, on the blank-looking sheet, you will see your handwriting appear. Now you can understand why, when fine print makes absolutely no sense whatever, in nine cases out of ten, *it is because instead of the original words, we are reading the foraging routes of Fine-Print Rotifers.*

This does not mean that FPRs are writing to us. It would be fun if their routes spelled out "Wassup?" or "Go Mets!," but that doesn't happen. They're eating, not writing. What's more, since the early nineteenth century (for reasons I'll explain) their foraging routes have become rigidly stereotyped, consisting of repeated groups of syllables. A typical example is one that I encountered during a dispute with my HMO. I'd had a operation on my eyes, and the HMO had denied my claim for the left eye. I called them and was told that they didn't pay for the same operation twice. I explained that it wasn't the same operation twice, but operations on two different eyes. I also explained that I used these two different eyes, "right" and "left," for my bicameral sense of vision. No go. I hung up the phone. I laid my head on the paperwork, then raised my head again, and tried to read page 12, section B, subsection B6.11, of my health insurance contract. Neither reading glasses, nor artificial tears, nor real tears, clarified page 12, section B, subsection B6.11, and in desperation I called my employer's benefits office.

"There's something wrong with my contract," I told the clerk, who said there could not be anything wrong with an individual contract as everyone was sent the same contract. "But," I told her, "I'm reading the terms of coverage right here, on page 12, section B, subsection B6.11, right at the bottom of the page?"

"I know where it is," she said.

"Well, on my contract, it says '*shnoo shnoo shnoo shnoo shnoo shnoo.*'"

"If that's what it says, that's what you're covered for," said the gal in benefits.

CONSIDER, NOW, THE RECENT subprime mortgage bubble in this context. Defaulting homeowners are blamed for signing contracts that they shouldn't have. Yet when people don't suspect that invisible rotifers have infested their mortgage contracts, how likely are they to question the fine print? Imagine a young couple, not well off, striving to impress a loan officer at a bank. Let's say they look at their contract before signing and try to understand it. Are they really going to mention the foraging route that I call "flock of ducks"? In such circumstances, would you feel comfortable saying to your banker, "Could you please explain what is meant by '*gegg egg wakwak gegg egg wakwak gegg egg wakwak?*'" Wouldn't you rather just sign? Consider, too, the scandal of robo-signing, so-called, which has swept the country in the wake of the housing crisis. Think of the millions of foreclosure cases in court, their files stuffed with mortgage assignments, satisfactions, affidavits, and other printed matter used to evict people from their homes—those potent papers which we have discovered to bear the same relation to reality as dark grimoires, invoking fantastical transactions signed by phantasmal bank officials never born of woman. This is not the work of human beings. This is the work of Fine-Print Rotifers, making themselves fat.

WHY DO FPRs EAT ONLY FINE PRINT? Tight-packed print affords them easier grazing, of course. But natural selection pressures, in the past, have also influenced their choice.

Long ago, FPRs grazed on many kinds of print and even ink blots. I have seen, in the library of my cousin who collects incunabula, an ancient Greek text emended by the great Renaissance scholar, Erasmus of Rotterdam, who believed that all humans were foolish and therefore should be loved, because even Christ was a fool—a holy one. In this fragile old book, Erasmus's name was inked out, wherever it appeared, by church officials who had disapproved of him, especially his notorious wedding of philosophy and religion in the prayer *O Sancte Socrate, ora pro nobis!* Over and over, Erasmus's name was blotted with a thick black stroke, so that future generations would not consider Socrates to be any kind of saint. But when I saw the book, those strokes had all but vanished, leaving only faint stains around the clear, sharp letters of Erasmus's name. It was wonderful to deduce, from this, the greed with which the Fine-Print Rotifers of the Renaissance had fallen on the censor's rich, thick ink. That they hadn't eaten Erasmus's name under the blots suggests that, by the time it appeared, the rotifers were gorged and glutted to the point where dessert excites only stifled moans. Through the next two centuries, FPRs continued to graze in the pastures of early modern print. Torrents of inked words in unpredictable spellings gave the rotifers an endless variety of specialized foraging routes. One has only to skim sixteenth- and seventeenth-century documents to hear, in imagination, the contented burps of rotifers finding treats around every *y* and *e*. I suspect that Fine-Print Rotifers even lent a hand, or cilium, to Shakespeare—*hey nonny nonny* sounds just like them.

But nothing lasts forever, and in the nineteenth century, the standardization of English spelling put a halt to that orgy of nourishment by severely restricting the rotifers' foraging routes. FPRs went through a decimation of all subspecies that had acquired orthographically messy routes as bad spelling was tossed into fireplaces, and hordes of English-eating rotifers suffered, for the sake of lunch, the fate of heretics. Natural selection favored those that consumed print less likely to draw critical attention—and what draws less critical attention than legal fine print? The Darwinian die was cast: evolution ensured the dominance of our modern FPRs.

They can also be found, though rarely, in books printed with double columns and small fonts. I have in my possession a double-column, Everyman's Library edition of Gibbon's *Decline and Fall* that exhibits FPR activity, shown below, in chapter XV.

> *Such is the constitution of civil society, that, whilst a few persons are distinguished by riches, by honours, and by knowledge, the body of the people is condemned to obscurity, ignorance, and* shnoo shnoo shnoo shnoo shnoo

—which spoils Gibbon's eloquence, but unwittingly underscores his somber point.

Cyclically Invisible Beasts

I

It's common knowledge that primates have an imitative streak. More surprisingly, so do fireflies. This is the only instance for which I can vouch of cyclical invisibility in the animal world: a case of invisibility proving to be so mixed a blessing that it is eventually abandoned for lesser evils, which, over time, become greater evils than invisibility's drawbacks, and so on. It is a bracing tale to ponder the next time you discover the light within yourself that nature put there to be seen.

Beacon Bugs

"Hᴀɪʟ, Hᴏʟʏ Lɪɢʜᴛ!" sang Milton. Who doesn't welcome light into a darksome world? Beacon Bugs, that's who. This native firefly species exhibits a unique feature: cyclical invisibility. They are invisible over periods of twenty-nine years; like cicadas, their cycle revolves around a prime number, the better to elude predators. (Beacon Bugs have a doozy of a predator to elude.) Then they produce one generation that outshines every other firefly species. For a few weeks, they are a glory, a far-flung, bedazzling beacon, a revelation of radiance, reminding themselves and all creation that an invisible firefly is a contradiction in terms and that if you make light, you should be seen. Humanity becomes aware of them at this point, and suffers the consequences.

All fireflies are creatures of incandescent romance. They cannot be bred in laboratories any more than love can. During courtship, the male offers his mate a gift of something nutritious—this isn't an entomology textbook, so let's call it chocolate. The happy couple deposits their eggs on the ground (not troubling with nest construction, free spirits that they are) and the larvae burrow, becoming glowworms, carrying the torch of firefly heritage almost from the moment when they were gleams in their parents' abdomens. And nothing, to a human eye, seems as dreamily romantic as the fireflies' mating flight.

The mating flight is a North American custom. Old World firefly courtships are sedate and communal: males fill up a tree and put on a light show, all together, to attract females (for some reason, one recalls the Red Army Chorus). On our shores, however, each male firefly goes for a solo evening cruise, flashing his tail lights over lawns, at dusk. You see glimmer-ribbons of fireflies hovering in a lovely layer, a few feet above the grass; you follow the floating sparks, living love letters scribbled on the dusk, begging, importuning a mate whose body, delicious, burning ripe, is hidden in the dimness. It's dark, you're still looking at the fireflies, you're thinking about how nice romance is and how the fireflies are all getting some, and being—forgive me—oblivious to the nightmare taking place under your nose.

A male firefly wafts over the tips of towering grasses, working his lights, flashing the code signal engrained in him for the sake of the rapturous moment when a female, receptive, eager, illumines herself in response. After a scintillating exchange, he tumbles from the air. He meets his bride. She flips him on his back, pinning him down with six pretty feet—she's bigger than he is—and proceeds to rip into his soft belly, tugging at his flesh, chewing with the steely mandibles of the predator genus *Photuris*. Her antennae vibrate with voracity; rude smackings echo through the grass roots. Poor lovelorn bug! He hasn't mated, he hasn't reproduced; he dies. She was the wrong kind. To her, he was just a piece of meat.

This scary proceeding is called "aggressive mimicry." Female *Photuris* fireflies mimic the mating flashes of other species' females, to trap and eat unwary males. *Photuris* is a real horror, a remorseless insecticide, a gothic subfamily curse, and the fatalest of femme fatales. To woo a female of his species, the *Photuris* male must trick her by imitating the flashes of another species' male—then, as the *Photuris* lady is getting out her (figurative) sushi knives, he drops his disguise and starts flashing dirty firefly talk. From a safe distance. If he's even sneakier, he imitates the *female* of another species. This draws the poor suckers of unwary males as well as the greedy *Photuris* girl, whetting her (figurative) kebab skewers. What happens? The *Photuris* male-in-drag ambushes the other males, opportunistically eats them, and then, taking every precaution . . . How tasteless.

Why don't the victimized fireflies change their mating signals? Oh, they do. North American fireflies continuously update their luminous codes, but what can I say—*Photuris* is an aggressive mimic, by definition, by inclination, and by vocation. She probably gets a kick out of cracking codes before dinner. Reader, look at your evening lawn, how it sparkles, flashes, and glimmers! A lagoon of love crisscrossed by pirates flying false colors, sowing deception, death, and the shipwreck of happiness, and all through the pure medium of light. It's July, but honestly, aren't your bare feet getting cold?

Beacon Bugs are the firefly species that has taken the most drastic step in self-defense. In each twenty-nine-year period, all generations of Beacon Bugs, except for one, are invisible. They can't be seen and they don't glow. Lights extinguished, the first invisible generations show a healthy population bulge, saved from the depredations of *Photuris* and her jerky boyfriends, as well as a host of other predators. My statistics heave a sigh of relief. But then they puzzle: instead of leveling off, the Beacon Bug population gradually declines. The last invisible generation is so thin on the ground it's practically decimated. Why should a powerful defensive strategy accompany the decline of the species it protects?

Some hypotheses come to mind. A firefly's flash can discourage predators who don't like a meal that blinds them. With the tactic of lightlessness, Beacon Bugs risk drawing predators that they haven't faced before. Invisible animals can see one another, and in spring, for example, the world is as full of invisible frogs and toads as it is lacking in charming princes. There's no free lunch, especially if you are lunch. Another hypothesis might

better explain the decline's gradualness. Like many fireflies, Beacon Bugs spend some two years in larval form,
underground. A lot can change in two years: a meadow
can be paved, dug up, flooded. When the larvae emerge—
well, have you ever driven around an unfamiliar neighborhood in the dark, without headlights, looking for
someone? Perhaps the newly adult Beacon Bugs have
trouble meeting up, and become gradually separated into
smaller, more vulnerable groups. Since, however, fireflies
are flying enigmas whose glow tantalizes the laboratories
that can't tame them, let's forget reasonable hypotheses.
Just for the argument, let's try love. If you were a Beacon
Bug, how would you feel about mating with somebody
who groped his way toward you, looking—not to put too
fine a point on it—like a cockroach? Maybe the Beacon
Bugs fail to multiply because they feel increasingly, pardon the expression, *turned off?*

With this in mind, let us ponder the scandalous wreck
of the luxury sloop *Folly*, which went aground and burned
on Niagara Reef in Lake Erie one cloudy summer night,
drowning the magnate Hoagland "Hog" Makemerry and
his young wife, Tipple. The family dragged the skipper
through a televised trial; long yarn short, he swore under
oath that he'd navigated toward the Toledo harbor light.
Not the gas buoy in the reef, no, the lighthouse beam,
he was certain. The bellies of viewing audiences shook
with laughter from Cleveland to Detroit. The prosecutor,
vengefully cordial, asked the skipper if he reckoned the

distance between the Toledo light and Niagara Reef? He did know the distance? Was the figure he said he knew in miles, or was it in feet? Oh, miles. Then he couldn't have seen the Toledo light, could he? Harrowed but curt, the defendant stuck to his story about a lighthouse beam, even after the bench's comment, which was, "Glug, glug."

"How shall I spell that, Your Honor?" asked the court recorder, deadpan amidst hilarity.

"You can spell that G, R, O, G."

The *Folly*'s skipper did see a lighthouse beam where none should have been. Now here is a curious fact about shipwrecks in Lake Erie: a ship goes aground almost exactly every twenty-nine years—the sandsucker *Isabella Boyce* off East Point Reef, 1917; the teak barquentine *Success* off Port Clinton, 1946; and so on. I would not be surprised if this pattern were found nationwide, from Maniticus to Point Reyes, along any North American coast where sailors tell of phantom lights that lure ships to their destruction, any coast with meadows and marshes where fireflies are hatched . . .

IT WAS A CLOUDY, MOONLESS NIGHT when the *Folly* followed the sweep, sweep, sweep of the beam penetrating the rough darkness. Who thinks twice about following that light unlike any other, a light that speaks our language, cheering us on? Even if a sailor was once a boy who collected fireflies in a jar, released them in a dark closet, and made them flash in synchrony with his flashlight, how could he imagine the swarms of desperate male Beacon Bugs coalescing by the thousands in the utter darkness along the *Folly*'s heading? How could he—how can any of us—fathom the promptings that compel a generation to break with the wisdom of its shadowy parents and grandparents and great-grandparents, and to throw itself ablaze in the midst of darkness, imitating the greatest lamp in its universe? Through the tragic night, the massed cloud of male Beacon Bugs, pressed to the limit, mad for love, threw off concealment and pulsed the brightest signal they could muster. To any passing ship, it looked like the light of harbor, of loving arms and home. Along the shores, female Beacon Bugs gathered in their myriads, what was left of them, and love-signals flashed from earth to sky, from sky to earth. The times had turned, the revolution had begun. And *Photuris*, eternal predator, surprised, pleased, added a long-missed item to her menu . . .

Washed up on the killer rocks of Niagara Reef, agape like a dead clam, lies a gold compact last held in the fingers of poor Tipple Makemerry; it used to reflect a human face, an animal face; now it reflects the cold cabal of the Pleiades. Desire for light, betrayal by light—how unholy it seems, yet how fitting and natural it is.

Epilogue

I

As this book began with a remembrance of my predecessor, Granduncle Erasmus, so I will end it with a nod to him, and a bow to his namesake, Erasmus Darwin, the grandfather of Charles Darwin, the founder of evolutionary theory. Erasmus Darwin wrote poetry about what was called, in his day, "natural history." My family is a cultured one, and Granduncle's parents named him in hopes that he would become equally adept with the microscope and the pen. Instead of turning out major discoveries along with volumes of verse, however, Granduncle turned out to see invisible beasts. But he always liked to quote his namesake's poetry, especially at Thanksgiving. As we'd sink into the after-dinner glow, Granduncle would suddenly stand up, shake out a pair of imaginary flounced cuffs, take a pinch of imaginary snuff, and intone:

> Glitter, ye Glow-worms, on your mossy beds;
> Descend, ye Spiders, on your lengthen'd threads;
> Slide here, ye horned Snails, with varnish'd shells
> Ye Bee-nymphs, listen in your waxen cells!

My own nonscientific reading has been less scintillating, but has inspired lifelong thoughts about nature; and in the spirit of Erasmus Darwin, I offer the following essay as an epilogue.

The Naturalist Reads a Love Letter, with Plato and a Dog

THERE ARE MANY WAYS for a thoughtful woman to read a love letter. I like to lie in bed while the rain is falling outside, with my knees drawn up under a quilt, my dog beside me, during one of those days that creeps along in crepuscular secrecy through the falling rain, which as it slackens, then resumes, creates a giddy sense of the height from which it falls . . . We float, my big old shepherd and I, in a nest of our making, with dreams atremble through his sleepy paws, those iron-clawed, knobby-toed paws as expressive as diaries; and me with a letter spread over my knees. A letter penned by the same animal hand that wants to touch me. How mysterious, the carnal magic in these lines. Between them, bit by bit, growing gradually more distinct, appear in miniature the figures and scenes of a very old, famous fable, all about love, and as it steals over my mind I am suddenly aware of curtains lifting, revealing what I've never seen before. My eyes are on the letter but my mind is following strange paths.

Do I still believe that there is no spiritual aspect of my life that is not, in some way, animal? It's the belief of a naturalist, a scientific observer of animals. I'm animal through and through. But how shall I apply my belief to the spiritual scent of this letter? I want to know (as women do) what love this is, here. And, maybe—what love is. A naturalist has one sort of truth; Cupid's knowing smile, an immeasurably different sort of truth . . . except, perhaps, in this fable that I grasp on the edge of dream, hopeful that if I follow it, I will understand the letter, and the lover, without diminishing any of the truths I live by.

THE FABLE WAS TOLD by a comedian at a party in Athens, very long ago. It had three parts and an introduction. The comedian, named Aristophanes, introduced it by burping, most likely with a look of mild gravity, as if he weighed each burp, its pedigree, its character, and its fitness for the job, before sending it out into the world. Then, with all the guests itching for a funny speech, he announced (to horny, vinous groans from some, and wry silence from others) that he would reveal the nature of love.

Once (he began), every human being was spherical, with two heads, four arms, and four legs. This spherical creature got around by cartwheeling, and was irresistibly powerful. It rolled to the top of the food chain, dominating the other animals, and from there it began threatening the gods, who punished it. They split it in half, "as you cut hard-boiled eggs with hairs," he said, and ever after, people have yearned to embrace their missing halves. Among the general laughter that greeted this, no one noticed (for science hadn't been invented) that this tale described the fertilized egg. Isn't that, now I see it, exactly what the spherical being is? Its double limbs are surely a diploid set of genes? The old fable has begun speaking to me as if it knew I was a naturalist. Let me see ... in the womb, the egg sits enthroned, potentially the most powerful of beings. Why? Because it has never heard or told a lie. It has never cringed, strutted, or lost sleep. It's going to roll out of there, into the path of whatever acts like a god, and try gamely to roll right over it. So this is what I think: when lovers yearn to be made whole in each other's arms, we yearn for our beginnings in that fine egg. Maybe that's why love rejuvenates, makes us rosy and frisky, feeling all the possibilities of life before us. That's what's so tempting ... and oh, doesn't my letter-writer know ...

But now, remember how Aristophanes, continuing, put a question to the partygoers.

"Look," he urged, "look at those couples—we all know them—who have been together for years. They want something from each other. What is it? We know it isn't just sex. Ask them and they can't tell you. It's a mystery." Heads nodded, glances met, tickled and solemn. The comedian then imagined that the smith-god offered one such loving couple the chance to be welded together into a single being. Of course, they jumped at the offer! Of course they would.

At this, the listeners smiled. At the notion of two lovers making one entity, like tin and copper in bronze, they smiled—not because the fable was unrealistic (these were sophisticated people) but because it showed love's power to make us forget our mortal, animal nature, so different from minerals and fire ... But maybe they missed something, those savvy partygoers for whom science hadn't been invented. Maybe ... the smith-god's offer *doesn't* make us forget our nature. What if this were true, instead, now that a chill is waving over my scalp—longtime lovers *remember* our elder nature, life's origin in nothing more promising than iron, sulphur, and fire. Yes.

Over the ocean floor stretches a desert lost in perpetual night, so barren it seems accursed. It's always in the back of my mind, for better or worse, with its name like a moaning wind, the *abyssal benthos*. And in it lie oases, places where volcanic cracks in the earth spew water that would be steam if three thousand meters of cold ocean weren't sitting on it. The water erupts blackly upward, a curdled tower, and all around it trembles a silvery, filmy mass of Pompeii worms, their little rear ends immersed in supercritically hot water, while their scarlet, feathery heads nod in the ambient cold water. The mood, way down there, is a cross between a nightclub and a fairy kingdom where banquets materialize out of nowhere. To the heavy-metal bass thumps of the earth's inner fires,

seven-foot-long tube worms of both sexes, also in scarlet
headgear, lounge around sending up shimmying eggs and
sperm bundles that find each other upcurrent. Shrimps
levitate over beds of juicy clams. Everyone lives it up
despite the total darkness that ought to make life impossible. Anywhere else on earth, light means life, energy,
photosynthesis, and the absence of the sun's blessed light
means barrenness. Anywhere except here in this dark
of darks. Why? Because there lives around the vent an
ancient form of bacteria that creates energy solely from
inorganic minerals like iron and sulphur. These bacteria take the place of sunlight: they are the vent's energy
source. They live inside the worms and feed them; they
carpet the vent and sustain its animals, and what is more,
the whole reason I began thinking about this is—*they are
smith-gods.* Sure they are! Because they forge life, animal
life, from the minerals and fires of our stony star. And in
so doing, they may have been, thousands of millions of
years ago, life's originators, the ones whose skill began it
all. Now I'm thinking of how uncanny it is that Venus,
goddess of love, was married to Vulcan, god of the forge.

The abyssal benthos. I whisper that eldritch name to
myself. I would give ... what would I give to see and
understand that place, those godlike beings, fully? I
would give my heart. And the yearning I feel is exactly
like something much more domestic, something at
which my letter writer daringly hints ...

The yearning of longtime lovers reaches beyond

the wholeness of the human egg, our beginnings, to the wholeness of all life's beginnings. Yes. I remember. Even when you want no more from your mate than a breakfast kiss, a pat on the shoulder, something yanks on you from an unsounded depth and demands the world! From every loving touch and kiss that lasts long enough also spreads, in a widening circle, a yearning to be made whole with all of life.

Bless him for reminding me, or damn him for it? Which? What sort of love is it? What is love? I believe . . . there is a third part of Aristophanes's fable, a hidden one, maybe the answer to my questions.

You have to know about him and those he entertained. The comedian had the most exquisite sense of limits an orderly mind can have. That's how he knew what was funny. He had a goal in life, and every year it was the same goal: to win first prize at the theater festival. That was enough for him, though not for his listeners, a circle of brilliant intellectuals seeking truth—at this particular gathering, they sought the truth about love. All night long, the guests delivered well-wrought speeches about love, in a spirit of rivalry pitched to high frequencies by the presence among them of a great eminence whose tongue had the power of slicing knees. When Aristophanes burped his introduction, it was a huge relief to those whose speeches had gone underpraised, or damned with faint praise, or had yet to pass their dry, wine-wetted lips. Only one guest noticed, however, that of all the speeches, the comedian's was the truest and best. That guest was none other than the eminent man himself, whose own speech—far and away the longest of the night—determined with the force of his world-historic intellect that love was a means to the perception of Ideal Beauty, which, whatever it was (and that is still disputed) had absolutely nothing to do with animal life. His speech was immortalized as it left his lungs. Still, he felt irked. By the time the guests had mostly left, the great man, red-eyed, was insisting that the best play-wright would be able to write tragedy as successfully as comedy. He flourished that claim through the air like an expert fly-fisher, but the comedian didn't bite. The funny man knew his limits. And I'd bet he knew that the shape of a comedy outlines the amorphous darkness of a trag-edy, as the nerves that convey a tickling sensation are the same pathways responsible for anguished pain. Aris-tophanes didn't bother answering the great philosopher, Socrates, because he knew his art.

Which leaves me with tragedy: the hidden, the untold, the painful part of Aristophanes's fable ... As a naturalist I see it coming, because, if the two comic parts smiled at our bodies and our loves, these things are also the stuff of terror. In our bodies, inside our cells, are bits of live ... things ... that our cells once tried to eat when they were small gobbling ameboids, millions of years before they formed our bodies. Our bodies consist of former ameboids with indigestible prey inside them.

These little Jonah-bits of gobbled but undigested former critters give my finger muscles the energy to move this page. Then there is sex. What is sex? "Thwarted cannibalism," says a famous biologist. You can say that again.

And I do. Thwarted cannibalism, I mutter. I smooth the paper lying across my quilt-covered knees, and as though the action of my palm brought invisible ink to light, it says: *I want to eat you up.*

He proposes to consume my time—which is the same thing—in the rites of the jealous domestic god who must be tirelessly satiated. Not that again. I will fail to locate in any of the kitchen cabinets the bottle of the special steak sauce, or the box of the special unsalted biscuits, that he must have, and there will be that catechism beginning, "How many times?" Or "How much intelligence?" Or maybe my misplaced binoculars—that I need *when* I need them—will be the excuse for his telling me, in detail stretching over an afternoon, how selfish I am. To such uses come the glorious human egg, and the font of life on the ocean floor. Is there a married woman who by the age of sixty hasn't acquired the stoicism of a gastrolith? To be fair, for every jaw-jutting Jove there's a jarring Juno. I don't care. To be frank, it's terrifying, this state of half-absorption into the gullet of another life.

Thwarted cannibalism and terror: is that the true name of this love? Of love itself? But tragedy is more than terror. It is pity, too, and ultimately it is mystery.

Muuuuuaaaaaaagh, moans my dog, opening his eyes

out of a dream in which he tried to bark, and could only squeak. Such a good dog, with those turret ears, now swiveling, silky as catkins, veined like rose petals, inside which the cartilage gyres downward in a smooth, ancient path. He loves a rub inside his ear. He'll press down on my thumb with his heavy head, eyes narrowed, like someone whose itch is a shade short of being scratched. Within the ear, it feels like touching a riddle, something sphinxlike, alive but inaccessible to my normal understanding; it makes me feel a discomfort that is the lowest grade of awe. Also, a rending pity for us both, frail animals, dependent on a touch here, a mercy there, and on the strange arrangement of kinship and killing that maintains us without our choice. I feel, now, the same pity for the author of the letter mutely insistent under the light of my bedside lamp.

What is love? Aristophanes said aloud, "Love is the name for the desire and pursuit of wholeness." But what he left unspoken, his words' tragic shadow, is a mystery that does not round off into wholeness, the happy marriage wrapping up a comedy. The desire and pursuit of wholeness lead us to embrace, in the form of a lover, our human birthright (that egg's promise), our heritage as living beings (those smith-gods' legacy), and—something more. Finally, we are led to embrace a mystery too great to encompass, as unending as nature because it is nature, the endlessness of the universe itself—that ultimate, unimaginable, ungraspable wholeness in which we are born and die, that haunts every intimacy. And that is why the letter I've read and reread cannot possibly hold, much less reveal, all it means. I cannot know. Love remains unknowable. In spite of all the nights spent together, in spite of the flavors that tongue and brain have cast in sensual bronze, in spite, even, of being each other's best friends. Love remains unknowable. Knowing that, the smile of Cupid deepens . . . and a naturalist, having sought truth, is satisfied with observation and hypothesis.

Acknowledgments

THIS BOOK BEGAN AS AN EXPERIMENT, so I am truly grateful to my mother, Marilyn Bentov, for encouraging its early stages, contributing her time, literary instincts, and critical faculties—and most importantly, her faith in my work. Thanks also go to Dr. Nancy Milburn for her kind and generous assistance with many fascinating sources, especially on the love lives of fireflies; and to Dr. Moira van Staaden and her family for her many helpful conversations. Susan Krueger provided inspiration with her Gulf War–themed quilt entitled *Pro Patria*. The Institute for the Study of Culture and Society, at Bowling Green State University, gave this book the time it sorely needed. My husband, Tom Muir, who calls screech owls out of the woods, showed me so much of what I have tried to put into words here.

I would also like to acknowledge the publications in which many of these stories originally appeared:

"The Antarctic Glass Kraken"
in *Stand*

"The Golden Egg"
in *The Kenyon Review*

"The Spiders of Theodora," as "Monumental City,"
   in *Orion*

"The Naturalist Reads a Love Letter with Plato and a Dog"
   in *Michigan Quarterly Review,* reprinted in *ISLE*

"The Couch Conch"
   in *Michigan Quarterly Review*

"The Oormz"
   in *Michigan Quarterly Review*

"Think Monkey"
   in *Michigan Quarterly Review*

"Feral Parfumier Bees"
   in *Ancora Imparo*

"Air Liners"
   in *Unstuck*

"The Wild Rubber Jack"
   in *Jewish Women's Literary Annual*

Bellevue Literary Press is devoted to publishing
literary fiction and nonfiction at the intersection of
the arts and sciences because we believe that science and
the humanities are natural companions for understanding
the human experience. With each book we publish, our
goal is to foster a rich, interdisciplinary dialogue
that will forge new tools for thinking
and engaging with the world.

To support our press and its mission, and for our full
catalogue of published titles, please visit us at blpress.org.

Bellevue Literary Press
New York